Cover Design and Interior Format

HIGHLAND LIES

THE BAND OF COUSINS

KEIRA MONTCLAIR

THE GRANTS AND RAMSAYS IN 1280S

GRANTS

LAIRD ALEXANDER GRANT and wife, MADDIE
John (Jake) and wife, Aline
James (Jamie) and wife, Gracie
Kyla and husband, Finlay
Connor
Elizabeth
Maeve

BRENNA GRANT and husband, QUADE RAMSAY
Torrian (Quade's son from his first marriage) and wife,
Heather—Nellie (Heather's daughter from a previous
relationship) and son, Lachlan
Lily (Quade's daughter from his first marriage) and husband, Kyle—twin daughters, Lise and Liliana
Bethia and husband, Donnan—son Drystan
Gregor
Jennet

ROBBIE GRANT and wife, CARALYN
Ashlyn (Caralyn's daughter from a previous relationship)
and husband, Magnus—daughter
Gracie (Caralyn's daughter from a previous relationship)
and husband, Jamie
Rodric (Roddy)
Padraig

BRODIE GRANT and wife, CELESTINA
Loki (adopted) and wife, Arabella—sons, Kenzie (adopted) and Lucas, daughter, Ami (adopted)
Braden and wife, Cairstine—son, Steenie (Cairstine's son
from previous relationship)

Catriona
Alison

JENNIE GRANT and husband, AEDAN CAMERON
Riley
Tara
Brin

RAMSAYS

QUADE RAMSAY and wife, BRENNA GRANT (see above)

LOGAN RAMSAY and wife, GWYNETH
Molly (adopted) and husband, Tormod
Maggie (adopted) and husband, Will
Sorcha and husband, Cailean
Gavin
Brigid

MICHEIL RAMSAY and wife, DIANA
David and wife, Anna
Daniel

AVELINA RAMSAY and DREW MENZIE
Elyse
Tad
Tomag
Maitland

CHAPTER ONE

———◆———

The Highlands of Scotland, Autumn, 1284

"STOP! STOP OR YOU'LL GO over the edge!"

Rose MacDole squealed as soon as she heard the deep male voice call out to her. She spun around in time to see the intruder heading straight for her. A big man, he was reaching out his hands as if to grasp her.

In a fit of fear, she spun on her heel and took off across the slippery rocks back toward her home, set high above the sea. She'd been warned not to speak with strange men. It was quite rare for her to even *see* a strange man because their castle was so isolated, and her mother preferred to stay at home.

The trek back to safety was not an easy one, but she'd traveled this path many times on her bare feet, just as she did now, running and glancing over her shoulder as the big man pursued her.

The best way to lose him was to follow the dirt path leading toward the sea, then sneak into the secret sea cave. Deep in its recesses was a secret door into the cellars of their castle, something her father had shown her years ago.

Down the path she scurried, sending rocks and debris over the side of the path into the sea, the sound of their journey a reminder of how far down she would fall if she lost her footing.

"Please stop! I'll not hurt you. I thought you were planning to jump over the edge. I only wanted to help."

He sounded sincere, but Rose could not forget the

warnings of the man she missed more than anything. Her dear sire, who'd passed on five years ago, leaving her alone with a mother whose moods were as violent and unpredictable as summer storms, had told her briefly about what men might ask of her when she grew into womanhood.

And her first, and only, experience with a kiss had ended badly for her. After that horrid event, her mother had ordered her to stay away from all men. Nay, she would not wait to see what he wanted. It would only end poorly for her.

Ignoring her mother always did.

Choosing her steps carefully, she hurried down the path, turning around occasionally to see if the man gained on her. He couldn't possibly catch her because she was more sure-footed than anyone along these cliff paths.

His voice echoed with the wind. "Stop, I demand you to stop before you get too close to the loch and it sucks you under."

Snorting, she wanted to ask him what he knew of her homeland, of their castle built on the cliffs overlooking the sea, where salt covered your skin and your clothing, and the air was as sweet as any she'd ever tasted. The castle overlooked a long loch that led to the firth and emptied into the sea eventually. It was known as Loch Linnhe, or *An Linne Dhubh,* the black pool.

She had been in and around the water as long as she could remember. Sometimes, she thought she was of the water.

Continuing down the path, she finally reached the bottom and raced around the point that brought her to the cave, the torch at the entrance lighting her way.

Her cave. She and her father used to come here together to sit in peace and quiet. It had always felt like a holy place, and they'd often talked to God and prayed in their private sanctuary.

Oh, if only she could enjoy those days again.

The man in pursuit of her didn't give up easily, still yelling at her to stop her forward progress. But she wouldn't. When she slipped into the cave, he'd have no idea what had become of her, the entrance too dark for him to see the secret door.

She counted her footsteps.

Breathing a sigh of relief, she slipped into the shadow of the cave, slowing her steps as she moved across the wet stone bottom. The stones overhead managed to glitter even in the dark. She was nearly at the door when his voice echoed inside the cave, the deep timbre bouncing off the cave walls. The man would not give up.

"Please, I just wish to help you."

The secret door was just ahead. The sound of his footsteps told her he was falling in behind her, unsure of the rocky bottom. She said a quick prayer for the Lord to guide her safely to her haven inside the door.

A minute later, she stepped inside the door, locking it behind her with a deep sigh of relief.

She'd made it.

So why did she feel a brief pang of regret?

———◆———

Roddy Grant struggled with indecision. He was unsure of whether to continue his pursuit of the lass whom he'd first seen on the cliff, looking as though she were about to leap to her death, or to give up and assume she'd probably relinquished her dark quest.

He stopped to gather himself, to slow the beating of his heart, and then decided to halt his pursuit. For now. Although he longed to help the girl, he was a stranger here, far from home, and it wouldn't do to break down the door.

This place was known as Loch Linnhe, the black pool, according to his cousin Braden, who'd taken over his wife's castle not far from here. How had it gained such an ominous name? Glancing over the edge, he answered his own question as he stared down at the darkness at the base of the caves, the sound of the water hitting the sharp rocks the only clue a loch sat beneath him. Being a sea loch, it was unlike the one he'd grown up on at the edge of his beloved Grant land. These were treacherous waters.

He'd come to be here on a mission for the Band of Cousins. His cousin Maggie had started the group with her husband Will. He and the others had dedicated their lives to putting an end to the despicable practice of selling humans across the water to other lands. Since then, they'd been able to save several bairns, lassies and laddies both, from their captors. Some were returned to their families, others adopted because their families hadn't wanted them.

After the cousins' last meeting, Roddy and his two Grant cousins, Connor and Braden, had decided to focus on the northwestern parts of Scotland. Roddy and Connor had drifted toward the coast with the intent of finding places where boats could land and take on human cargo. Braden had not joined them on this trip because he was newly wed, but he'd accompany them on the next jaunt.

Their journey had led him toward this castle. It was a small one not far from Sona Abbey, so it was entirely possible that it supported a small family instead of a clan. The rocky terrain was not likely to grow many crops, though one could build a small garden.

They'd almost decided not to investigate the castle due to its negligible size, but Roddy had been drawn there by some inexplicable force. He'd insisted on taking a closer look while Connor rode on to explore another area. They would meet later.

From a distance, they hadn't known the castle sat directly on Loch Linnhe, which made it a point of interest for the Band of Cousins. Braden had told him the loch wasn't far, which was exactly why they'd headed in this direction, but he hadn't mentioned the castle.

From a distance, they hadn't seen *her*.

Roddy skidded and wobbled his way back across the dangerous landform to the cliff he'd been standing on when he'd first seen the lass. The castle was quite beautiful, but it was completely surrounded by water on three sides, perched high above multiple rocks and cliffs, which were presumably too steep for invaders to use as points of attack. Roddy stood a short distance away, the early autumn breeze cooling him, thinking of the lass.

The image of her standing there would stay with him always. The lass was gloriously beautiful, her hair so dark, it could be called black. Long strands had escaped her braid, whipping in the wind as she stared down at the tumultuous waters beneath her.

Had she really been intent on throwing her life away?

Or had he only thought so because that idea of tumbling from the cliffs had been on his mind as he stood overlooking the rough, brutal waters of the dark sea? True, he hadn't considered jumping to his death—quite the opposite—but those who knew him would be surprised to hear the unusual direction his thoughts had taken.

The fear of death had niggled at the back of his mind for as long as he could remember, but it had roared to life after his uncle Alex, the greatest warrior in the Highlands, was nearly cut down in battle. Watching Braden fight in their most recent battle had stirred his fear even more, so much so he could no longer ignore it. In fact, the fear had grown so strong that he pondered requesting not to fight as a Clan Grant warrior in the future.

But what would his clan think of him then? Every lad dreamed of becoming a fine warrior, especially if they could fight for one of the strongest forces in all of the Highlands.

The recurrent dream of drowning in deep water that assailed him night after night only made matters worse, forcing him to wonder what exactly had brought all of this upon him.

Had his nightmares somehow pulled him here to Loch Linnhe? Did the black pool have a message for him? No matter how much he searched his mind for answers, he came up empty.

Then the lass had appeared, distracting him from his thoughts.

He made his way back to the main path he'd followed before pursuing her. He would go to the castle. Since his goal was to patrol the area, it would be courteous to introduce himself—to go to the gates and request entrance in the name of Clan Grant—and it would also allow him to inquire after the girl.

To his surprise, the guard at the gates allowed him in without much of an interrogation. After the stable master took his horse, he made his way to the keep, surprised to see a woman awaiting his arrival.

She was tall and thin, her dark hair pulled into a tight bun. "Come inside, young man. How can I assist you? Are you lost? 'Tis not often we have visitors to our cliffs." Her broad smile appeared sincere and she beckoned him inside with a wave of her hand. As he followed her through the door, she turned quickly to address a serving lass. "Please find a simple repast for our guest. I'm sure he has quite a thirst, wherever he is from."

Roddy took a brief glance around the great hall, at the rich tapestries, the weaponry, the rich woodwork. This was a castle built from great wealth. "I'm from Clan Grant."

"Clan Grant?"

"Aye, of Dulnain Valley."

"Then you are quite a distance from home. Have a seat, lad."

Roddy sat at the nearest trestle table, accepting the ale and bread brought by the serving lass. He waited for the woman to take a seat in a cushioned chair near the table before he spoke. "I hope I'm not prying, but I was drawn by the sea, and I found my way to a cliff just south of your castle. I happened to see a young lass standing in a precarious position. I feared she was about to leap or fall to her death. Do you know of her?"

"A young lass about to leap to her death?" Her hand moved to her throat in shock. Moments later, her expression relaxed. "Oh, you must have seen my daughter, Rose, but she would never attempt such a thing. She loves to walk out across the cliffs and has been doing so since she was a bairn. She's as surefooted as any animal, trust me. You must have seen her during her morning walk. She's such a sweet thing. Believe me, she was not about to leap to her death. The girl just loves the sea, and the more the waves pound against the rocks, the longer she remains. I never worry about her on the bluff. Her sire taught her how to cross the cliffs many years ago. 'Twas their morning ritual." The woman waved her hand to the serving lass and said, "Please ask Rose to join us."

She smiled again and said, "I'll let you see her with your own eyes if you are so concerned."

He nodded, listening to the woman's slight English accent. What would have brought an Englishwoman so far north in the Highlands? "My thanks," he said. "I would feel better if I saw she was hale with my own eyes. I'm Roddy Grant. And you?"

"Oh, my pardon. I'm Jean MacDole. My husband Walter passed on several years ago. Rose and I have struggled with his loss. She walks the cliffs to keep her father's memory fresh in her mind. We both adored him." Her eyes misted as her hands fell into her lap. "Young man, you need not be concerned. Now tell me why a Grant lad is in our area."

"Just traveling north. My cousins and I enjoy traveling, meeting new people and making connections with other clans. We have a cousin who is now in Muir Castle, so we wished to get to know his neighbors."

"You're a distance from Muir Castle."

"Mayhap a half day's ride or less. Are there any large

clans in the area?"

"A few. But I do not associate with them. If you cannot tell, I am English. Our marriage was arranged, and I did as I was told to do. Fortunately, Walter and I grew to love each other. And our sweet Rose is the result of our dear love. Ah, here she is now."

She smiled and stood to greet her daughter, who'd grown wide-eyed as soon as she entered the hall. Her gaze had gone to her mother briefly, but now it remained on Roddy. Her eyes were a haunting shade of dark blue, nearly purple. When had he ever seen eyes that color?

Roddy also stood, then took a step closer to her, a strange force compelling him. "Greetings to you, my lady. My apologies if I frightened you a few moments ago. 'Twas not my intention, but I feared for your safety. 'Tis a long way down to the turbulent loch. You call the sea loch the black pool, aye?"

She smiled, a beautiful but hesitant smile. Her hair showed evidence of her travel outside on the cliffs. The strands of hair he'd seen whipping in the wind now fell in soft curls about her face. She had lips that matched her name, as rosy as they came. He waited for her answer, but she stared at the floor.

"Are you hale? You were not hurt on the rocks? I thought you were barefoot. Those craggy rugs must have been mighty sharp on your tender skin."

Still she did not reply, instead wiggling her toes in the soft blue slippers now on her feet. She wore a dark blue gown that set off her eyes. Roddy had to admit he'd never been as taken with a lass's appearance as he was with hers. How he wished to touch the soft skin of her cheek or have one sweet taste of her lips. But more than anything, he wanted her to tell him she was fine—not because he worried about her health, but because he wished to hear her voice.

Would the tone be low and husky? Would it be high and

soft?

How could he get her to answer him?

He'd ask her a question that required an answer instead of a simple nod of her head.

"What was that path you followed?" When she didn't respond, he forged ahead. "And what is your favorite flower?" Ridiculous, but he couldn't think of anything else that would force her to speak.

Her mother replied, "My lord Grant, my daughter is deaf and does not speak."

CHAPTER TWO

ROSE HAD TO LISTEN TO her mother lie. This was her destiny. She was to allow everyone to believe she could not hear simply because she could not speak.

Sometimes it was a blessing, but in this case, she wished she could converse with the man standing in front of her. Her disability *did* allow her to stare at people at will, something she was rarely questioned about, and she used that to her advantage now to watch this fair-haired man who stood close enough to touch.

While she had feared him out on the cliffs, now she was simply intrigued. Ever since her sire had died, her mother had kept to the castle, only leaving to visit the kirk or the abbey for prayer. She left Rose at home so as not to subject her to people's natural curiosity about a girl who could neither speak nor hear. Or so she said. They had an occasional visitor, but Rose was rarely invited to join her mother. Most of her time was spent either outdoors or in her chamber.

Her solitary existence hadn't bothered her in the thick of her grief for her sire—years had passed without her hardly noticing—but her life had begun to seem empty to her of late. Hollow. This man had traveled the Highlands. Oh, the stories he must have!

She hadn't gotten a good look at him out on the cliffs, but he was also quite handsome, with sun-kissed hair and gray eyes—eyes that reached into her soul. Something told her he wasn't a danger to her after all, that, indeed, he might be a friend.

But only if she could find a way to communicate with him away from her mother's watching eye.

His skin was bronzed by the sun, and he had a strong, chiseled jaw with a scar just above his right eye, so close it was a wonder he hadn't been blinded by whatever had damaged his skin enough to leave a deep scar.

It didn't distract from his attractiveness at all, instead making him a bit more appealing.

Rose suspected she'd been granted special insight into the people around her to make amends for her impairment. When she spent time around someone, she could intuit things about them—what they were like, whether their behavior met their words. She'd been hiding around the corner so she knew this man's name was Roddy Grant. Roddy or Rodric, she guessed, had a strong character, the appearance of a warrior, and a powerful sense of pride and honor. She only sensed such unmitigated confidence in one of every four or five people. It always made her wish to know the person better.

She also sensed something else. Roddy Grant was a troubled man. She tipped her head, attempting to pick up more clues about him. He seemed to feel guilty, but that was all she could discern.

This is how she entertained herself around strangers. She couldn't communicate with them, so she spent her time observing them, hoping to find clues to their character in the way they carried themselves, spoke to others, and acted. Rose was surprised when Roddy gave her a slight bow, indicating he would be leaving, and thanked her mother for her hospitality.

She didn't want him to go. She didn't want to lose sight of that sun-kissed hair or those expressive eyes. How she wished she could beg him to stay or promise to meet her for a short interlude on the cliffs or in the gardens. Now that she'd met him, she had one burning desire.

She wished to know what Roddy Grant had done to

make himself feel guilty.

———◆———

Roddy had to admit, he'd never been more surprised than when Lady MacDole had announced that her daughter was deaf and mute. He'd instantly felt sorry for the poor lass. Though he didn't presume to know anything about the lass, her life had to be lonely. She was cut off from the rest of the world not just by her location and her small family, but also by the fact that nature had robbed her of speech and hearing, both invaluable to communication. He couldn't help but wonder if she'd been that way since birth or if she'd lost her hearing and speech in some tragic accident.

Even as he left the great hall, he knew his business there was not done. He would search for answers. He told himself it wasn't her beauty that drove him but rather the wish to help her. After all, his own mother, Caralyn, was the Grant healer, a calling she'd learned from his aunts Jennie and Brenna Grant, two of the most renowned healers in all of Scotland. He was glad for his mother's knowledge. He often had many questions to ask her.

He left the isolated castle and made his way back to the clearing where he and Connor had agreed to meet when the sun was high. He was a wee bit early, but Connor stood there munching on an apple, a satchel filled with the ripe fruit now hanging from his saddle bag. His horse chomped down on his own treat.

"Successful journey?" Connor asked in between chews.

"Nay, certainly not."

"You're quite pensive about something," Connor noted.

Roddy let out a deep sigh. He could hardly make sense of his own thoughts, but perhaps Connor could help him work through them. He, Connor, and Braden had been friends for as long as they'd been alive. Even better that they were cousins.

There was only one thing he'd knowingly kept from Connor. The last son of the renowned warrior Alexander Grant, Connor loved going to battle.

Would he comprehend Roddy's fear of dying?

Mayhap it was time to find out. *After* he told him about the oddity of Rose MacDole's situation and the fact that her castle overlooked Loch Linnhe. "I strayed over the cliffs near the castle and saw a young lass standing near the edge."

Connor's arched brows told him he'd caught his interest.

"I followed her, but she ran. Not surprising because I'm clearly a stranger, but she was sure of foot and outran me. I had to go to the gates to gain entrance and see what she was about." He crossed his arms and stared at the deep violet flowers not far from his feet, noticing how close they were to the color of Rose's eyes.

"And then?" Connor was a good listener, just like his father. Roddy wished it were a trait he shared, but he lacked patience, and more often than not, he'd begin peppering the speaker with questions partway through the telling of the tale.

"The castle was owned by a Walter MacDole, who passed on several years ago, and is now occupied by his widow and daughter, Rose. Rose being the one I saw on the cliffs. I didn't see many others…a guard at the gate, one serving lass, and a stable master."

Connor took another bite of his apple, talking with his mouth full. "Usually meeting a young lass puts a smile on a lad's face. Why does your expression tell me otherwise? Was she homely?"

Roddy whistled. "Far from homely. She was quite a beauty with dark hair, nearly black, and eyes nearly the color of those." He gestured to the flowers he'd noticed.

"And this disturbs you?" Connor now sported a sly grin.

Roddy smiled himself, knowing how his cousin would react when he filled him in.

He caught Connor's gaze. "That did not disturb me. It was finding out that the lass cannot hear or speak that troubled me."

"Truly?" The shock on Connor's face was exactly the reaction he'd expected. His cousin stared at the ground, working over this new information. "How would you know she was deaf if she could not tell you so?"

"Her mother told me."

"So you accepted this." Connor paused, staring into the trees before he spoke again. "Why does it bother you?"

"I cannot explain it, but something about her situation is not right. The castle sits on the sea loch Braden told us about. Loch Linnhe describes the water quite accurately— dark and turbulent. I could see from the cliffs. That may be another reason to go back."

His cousin settled his hands on his hips and took two steps closer. "Because you saw something that made you believe it could be part of the Channel of Dubh?"

The Channel of Dubh was the main network they and their cousins had been pursuing. A loosely organized group that captured lads and lassies and then sent them off, never to be seen again.

He shrugged. "Mayhap. 'Twould take a big boat to handle those treacherous waters." If he wished to share his problem with Connor, the time had come. Roddy ran his hand through his hair and took a deep sigh as if that extra breath could force the words from his lips. "There is something else I wished to ask your opinion about. I've had nightmares of late."

Connor quirked his brow at his cousin. "Go on."

"I dream I'm submerged in water and am fighting to get to the surface, fighting for air." He began to pace, hoping to get the courage to say even more. "I…I've apparently developed this unusual fear of dying. Ever since your sire…"

Connor held his hand up. "Say no more. I understand.

I went through something similar myself, but 'twas short-lived. When we rode into battle against Buchan, I was certain I'd be struck down, just like my sire. Before the battle, I kept dreaming I was the one lying wounded on the field before Grant Castle."

"You did?" He couldn't have been more surprised to hear those words from the son of Alex Grant.

"Aye, but as soon as I actually swung my sword again, the fear disappeared."

Roddy apparently did a poor job of hiding his disappointment because Connor quickly added, "The same hasn't happened for you, I'm guessing."

Roddy rubbed the heels of his hands against his eyes. Why couldn't he just erase the fears from his mind? "Nay. My fear of dying in battle hasn't changed, and my nightmares have only gotten worse. When I looked across that dark water, the churning depths mesmerized me."

"Is that the kind of water you see when you wake up after a nightmare?"

Roddy thought for a moment before he answered, considering the sights and sounds he remembered from his night terrors. "Nay, my sense is the water is calm. 'Tis nothing like Loch Linnhe, yet I'm drawn to return to the castle, the water. Something is pulling me back."

Connor moved over to his horse, patting his flank. "I would never question your instincts. I think we should return."

"To see if I recognize anything from my dream?"

"Nay, I think we should sneak down to the water to look for a landing for boats. 'Tis why we are here, aye? From your description, it could be the perfect place for those black-hearted wretches to load their captives. The woman and the young lass up on the cliff may have no idea what transpires beneath their home. We'd be remiss if we didn't explore more, search out anything unusual." Then he winked at Roddy. "And if we happen to see the young lass, all the better. She could be what's pulling you back, not the water. I would love to meet her, see what I make of her."

Roddy grinned. He had hoped that Connor would suggest returning. "Makes perfect sense to me. I doubt we'll get inside the castle again, but there's a sea cave below, one she disappeared into when I was following her. If the sun drops, it could light up the area around the cave for us." He moved over to his horse to mount up. "Did you find anything of interest at the castle where you stopped?"

"Nay, there is naught to concern us there. I suspect fate brought us to MacDole Castle—and a beautiful lass. I hope we see her."

———◆———

Roddy and Connor headed back toward Loch Linnhe, and they opted to go straight to the front gate to start their search. Dusk was upon them, so Roddy feared they'd be turned away, but they were allowed in.

A man greeted them at the door to the hall. "Were you not here earlier today, lad?"

"Aye, my name is Roddy Grant, and this is my cousin, Connor Grant. I did not meet you earlier."

The man's gaze focused on him, narrowing just a touch. "Nay, you did not. I am Harold Caswell, steward of Mac-Dole Castle. May I be of assistance?"

"We'd like to speak with Lady MacDole and her daughter Rose," Roddy said. "We have some questions for them."

Caswell glanced off to the side before returning his gaze with his answer. "The ladies have retired for the evening. If you have a question, you may ask me. I have permission to speak for Lady MacDole. You are aware that her daughter is unable to answer you, if I recall."

"Aye," Roddy glanced at Connor before responding. "We are seeking information about any shipments made from here. Have you ever witnessed any unusual occurrences on the sea loch? Mayhap a ship docking nearby in the night? A small boat carrying too many people? Any unusual noises at night?"

Harold shook his head vehemently. "I've never heard any ships at night. It is quite preposterous for you to suggest such activities could take place near our land without us knowing. My answer is nay, so you may take your leave. You'll find nothing of that sort here."

Connor said, "Many thanks to you. We'll take ourselves away."

The seneschal nodded and spun on his heel before heading back into the castle.

As soon as the man was far enough away, Connor said, "I agree with your instincts. Something is not right here."

They retrieved their horses from the stable and left through the front gate so as not to arouse any suspicion. As soon as they were out of view, Roddy said, "I'm going back to the cliffs. I have to see if Rose came back."

"I'll follow," Connor said. "If you find her and wish to speak with her, I'll stand guard for you. See if you can learn anything, though I don't know how since she cannot hear or speak."

"No need to guard me. Do your own investigation of the area. I'll find you later."

Connor nodded. "Suits me. I'll find my way down to the water. I'd like to see for myself if there are any docks or moorings. Join me when you've finished whatever 'tis you're searching for at this hour." He chuckled and patted Roddy on the back before he took off down the path and disappeared from sight.

He'd join Connor when he could because he agreed there could be something afoot at the sea loch, but first he had more pressing issues.

He had to see Rose. If he saw her one more time, his interest would be assuaged. He was certain of it.

CHAPTER THREE

———◆———

ROSE SAT ON HER FAVORITE rocky ledge on the lower cliff overlooking the sea. She loved to listen to the rolling waves when the weather was rough. The sound of the crests as they crashed against the large rocks at the coastline reminded her of the time she'd spent here with her sire, watching as the white caps broke apart into a thousand bubbles and the seagulls and pelicans soaring overhead dived for their quarry. Her favorite bird was the pelican. It had the amazing ability to fly nearly vertically after its prey. It would then surface quickly with a deep swallow, telling her its dinner had begun. Her sire had taught her all about their feathered friends, his favorite being the owl.

But as much as she enjoyed watching the birds and soaking in the natural beauty of the sea and its cliffs, her mind was distracted by the memory of a pair of gray eyes. Could Roddy Grant help her? Though she loved her home, she was tired of being lonely. She'd thought of running away, but she had no idea where she could go.

Fear of her mother's retaliation also kept her home. She was isolated, a prisoner of sorts, due to both her disability and her ignorance of the world around her.

There had to be more to life than dreaming on a cliffside outcropping.

How she wished her mother had allowed her the opportunity to learn to read. Her sire had brought books home from the abbey on occasion. He'd shown her letters and words, ensuring she could recognize numbers and all the letters of the alphabet, but her mother had put a stop to the lessons. She'd declared the tasks too stressful for Rose, but Rose knew the real reason.

Her mother wished to have complete control over her daughter and everything that transpired in the castle. It had been a constant tone of discord between her parents.

Now, Rose was marooned in a world where she couldn't communicate with others, a world of silence and frustration.

Now that her father was gone, her mother had seen to it that she had no contact with the outside world.

She heard a rock fall over the ledge and caught something out of the corner of her eye. Jumping to her feet, she saw someone was making his way toward her across the cliffs.

Roddy Grant.

This time she took a tentative step toward him instead of running away. It was time to stop running away. As soon as they met up, she cautiously smiled.

"Can you read my lips?" Roddy asked.

She didn't answer, instead reaching for him. It felt important for him to know the truth. If he did, mayhap he could help her. Daring to do something she'd never done before, she grabbed his hand, pulling him closer, and began motioning to him. She tugged on her ear, nodded, then held her finger to her lips as if to quiet him.

"I guess that's my answer. How I wish you could, Rose. There's something odd about your life, your mother, your steward, something I wish to examine. I could use your help."

Her heart gave a lurch, a feeling akin to hope. He hadn't understood her silent message, but he was clearly interested in her well-being.

"I'd hoped you could tell me something." He started to turn away, but she grabbed his arm.

She wouldn't lose this chance. Holding his hand steady,

she tugged her ear again, nodding, pleading with him to understand her.

"I don't understand. If you cannot hear, why are you tugging on your ear?"

Rose shook her head and pointed to his mouth, then her ear, and nodded again. She brought her index finger from her ear and then pointed to his face, nodding.

"What? You could hear once?"

She shook her head with such emphasis that the truth finally dawned on him. She could see it in his gaze.

He cupped her cheek and whispered, "You can hear me?"

She nodded, a broad smile breaking out across her face. She pointed to her mouth and shook her head.

"You can hear, but you cannot speak?"

She nodded again, filled with the joy of being understood, and couldn't help but give him a brief hug before stepping back.

"Why did your mother lie?"

Rose thought hard about some of the things her sire had taught her, then traced the letter S on her chest, mouthing the word slowly to him.

"It's a secret? But why?"

Then she pointed to the castle and formed the word "mother" with her lips.

"Your mother wishes it to be a secret?"

When she nodded quickly, he looked befuddled and whispered, "Truly? Why would she do such a thing to you?"

Rose dipped her head and closed her eyes, her embarrassment at her own mother's treatment of her suddenly too much. Memories of her accident flitted through her mind like fireflies, but she chose to ignore them, not wishing to recall anything about it—it was simply too painful. She could feel the blush rise to her cheeks. Maybe she should walk away. A tear formed on her lash, so she turned away, swiping it from her face.

All she'd wanted was a friend.

Roddy circled around her, stilling her with a gentle hand on her shoulder. "Nay, you'll not leave me after that revelation. I wish to know more, Rose. Something odd is going on here. I'm not sure if you're involved, but if so, I'd like to help. What can you tell me?"

His brow arched in a way that stretched the scar near his eye. She wanted to ask him how he had gained such a mark, but she couldn't. Her hand reached out for his cheek and he took a step closer before freezing in place, his gaze locked on hers as the tips of her fingertips touched his flesh.

She gasped at the contact. His skin was warm and rough from his shorn beard. She retreated with uncertainty, but he nodded and reached for her hand, cupping it inside his and bringing it back to his cheek.

"Don't pull away. I like your touch. Your skin is verra soft." He smiled and she sighed at how handsome the smile made him, his white teeth shining in the dark of the night.

Deciding to be bold, she took a step closer and brought her thumb up to trace the scar near his eye. She rubbed across the shiny skin, now pale against the bronze of his sun-darkened face, and arched her brows in question at him.

"Ah, my scar puzzles you." He rubbed the back of his hand down her cheek. "The oddest part of that scar is I don't recall how I earned it. Probably sparring with one of my cousins. I have many of them and we loved swordplay at a young age."

She slowly moved her lips just as he had, "Cousins?" though no sound came out.

"Aye, I have many male cousins, and we all fought to be just like our sires and uncles. We practiced to be warriors so we would be ready to fight to defend our clan when the time came." He was quiet for a long moment, as if considering something, then said, "I don't know how or why, but mayhap however I came by this scar is the reason I have a fear of dying." He stared off at the moon, his eyes darkened with pain. "Every time battle is imminent, fear takes away my ability to think, to reason, to keep my emotion in check. 'Tis most dangerous, that much I know."

Fascinated with this man, she nodded, encouraging him to continue.

He said, "I'm a warrior for one of the strongest Highland clans, the Grants, and I'm scared every time I draw my sword. I watched my cousin Braden in the last battle we fought, and I could have heaved from watching the risks he took. What if I get sick in front of all the other warriors? What if I pass out or drop to the ground in fear? I'll tell you, I'd be an embarrassment to my sire and my uncle and my cousins…"

He paused, his hands now on his hips, his gaze on the rocks below. Had he assumed she was contemplating a jump because he'd considered taking his own life? The thought made her shudder.

She continued to gaze at him, giving him the opportunity to ease his burden if speaking his fear aloud could do that. Though he was clearly ashamed, she imagined the fear he felt was quite normal. Her sire had fought a battle in England, and he'd often told her about how it had affected him.

"If I embarrass my clan, I'll be forced to go into hiding, which I do not want. My only hope is that I'll be able to hide my fears well." He jerked his gaze back to hers, his hand now moving up to her cheek. "My thanks to you for listening." He brushed the back of his hand across her cheek. "You have no idea how beautiful you are, do you, Rose MacDole?"

She shook her head briefly to indicate she was confused, so he cupped her cheeks and said, "You are so beautiful that I long to kiss you. Would you allow it?"

She nodded, certain that this kiss would be different from the first kiss she'd experienced, one that had been forced upon her. He stepped closer and wrapped his arms around her. A brisk wind came up and the hoot of an owl called to them. Roddy was so handsome he nearly took her breath away.

His lips descended on hers. She didn't know how to react but followed his lead, moving the same way he did. His tongue touched the seam of her lips and she parted them hesitantly, surprised at the feel of his tongue invading her mouth. Surprise turned to passion as she got her first taste of this man, as sweet as a freshly picked apple. An odd sound came from Roddy, much like the growl of an animal, and he tugged her closer, the hard planes of his abdomen and his chest melding with her curves so they almost felt as one person. Her cheeks grew warm, and her breathing turned raspy and out of control. Sadly, he ended the kiss rather abruptly, but then gave her two more soft kisses.

"Rose MacDole, you make me take leave of my senses. I came here to meet you but for another reason as well." She lost her balance when they separated, her knees weak, but he caught her. "I'm glad I affect you as well."

Saddened that they had separated, she reached up to touch the heat of his lips. Still, she knew it wasn't wise to be outside with a strange man. If her mother were to see them...

"My cousin Connor headed down to explore the shoreline of the loch. Would you take me down there? We're on a mission. Boats are selling cargo from a loch in this area, and we wish to see if 'tis this one."

She nodded and took his hand, leading him down the path that led to the cave. This time she took a different turn when they were nearly at the base of the cliff. They hadn't gone far when the outline of a tall man appeared in the moonlight.

Rose pivoted and mouthed, "Your cousin?"

"Aye, 'tis Connor."

They found their way over to him and took him by surprise, the noise of the waves drowning out the sound of their approach. Roddy introduced them, and Rose gave him a warm smile. He was taller than Roddy, though not as handsome. His hair was as dark as hers.

Roddy quickly added, "Rose can hear you, but she cannot speak. I'll explain later."

Connor quirked his brow, glancing at his cousin, but rather than comment, he turned to her and said, "Rose, there's a dock just a bit south of here. Do you ever see it used?"

She nodded, pointing to the moon. Connor glanced at Roddy, apparently confused. "At night?" he asked. "You've only seen it used at night?"

Roddy moved to stand in front of her. "Do you use it? Your steward?"

She shook her head and then shrugged her shoulders, hoping her meaning came through. Her steward didn't use it, but she didn't know who did.

"We're going to ask you a few questions," Roddy said. "Just indicate aye or nay." He still held her hand, and she was pleased he hadn't stopped this small intimacy when they came upon Connor.

It made no sense given their short acquaintance, but Roddy Grant made her feel safe and protected.

He continued, "How often do you see a boat?"

Roddy shook his head and said, "Aye or nay, Connor. Do they come once a sennight?"

She shook her head.

"A fortnight?"

She indicated aye.

"Do you know the men?"

Another head shake.

Connor started. "Have you seen what they put in the

boat?"

She indicated nay.

Connor said, "She probably cannot see from her castle."

She widened her gaze, pointing to the moon again.

"It always comes late at night?" Roddy interpreted. "How can they see?"

Rose put both hands on her head in a round shape and turned in a full circle.

Connor muttered, "I don't know what she means. Try again?"

"A beacon," Roddy cried out. "Correct?"

Rose nodded, excited they'd understood her without much effort.

In the distance, she heard a voice calling her name. She pointed, indicating she had to leave. It was her mother's steward, Harold, and she didn't wish for him to see her with the two men.

"I'll escort you, Rose."

She shook her head vehemently and spun around, but Roddy said, "Wait."

When she turned to face him again, he leaned down and placed a tender kiss on her lips, one that made her wish to melt against him, but her name rang out across the stones.

"Rose, I promise we will meet again someday."

As she hurried up the path to the caves, her fingers shot up to touch the spot on her lips where he'd kissed her. He'd given her more than he would ever guess.

Roddy Grant had given her something she hadn't imagined possible.

He had just given her hope.

———◆———

Roddy waited until he and Connor were back outside the gates of the castle, far enough away not to be noticed. Shaking his head, he chastised himself for not being more observant. He should have noticed that Rose could hear.

She'd known he was coming both times he'd discovered her on the cliffs.

But it didn't matter. He was so pleased they had a way to communicate he couldn't stop the smile he carried on his face or in his heart. Hell, but this lass had gotten to him in a short time.

"She's a beauty indeed, cousin," Connor said with a wink and a sly grin.

"She's a bonnie lass…and sweet and strong. I don't know what goes on here, but I'd like to find out," Roddy said, looking dejected. "Makes me a wee bit sad. 'Tis possible I may never see her again, though I'll do everything in my power to do so."

"Would you court a lass who cannot speak?"

"Mayhap not, but 'twould be nice to know her better."

Connor gave him a knowing look. "You cannot ignore the pull she has on you."

He only grunted in reply as they mounted their horses and headed inland.

"Now that I've given it more thought," Connor said, "I think we should stop at the abbey I visited shortly after we left Braden's, Sona Abbey. You traveled to another small castle while I was there." He paused, as if considering the matter, then added, "Both of us have sensed something is not right at MacDole Castle. I had a similar response to the abbey. I dismissed it at the time because 'twas my first trip there. Now, I fear I may have missed something."

"The abbey is not that far from MacDole Castle," Roddy offered, putting voice to what they were both thinking.

"Aye, which makes me wonder if there's a connection to the MacDoles. I'll say no more than that. You give me your opinion once we arrive."

Roddy agreed, so they mounted and headed toward the abbey.

Even though a small part of him hated leaving Rose behind, he wondered if anything could come of a relationship with her, especially with an overbearing mother who lied about her daughter's abilities. What kind of cold beast would tell everyone Rose was deaf when she wasn't? On the surface Jean MacDole had appeared a kind—if cold—woman, but he couldn't imagine any of the women he knew from Clan Grant treating their child with such callous disregard. He couldn't rid himself of the unease he felt about the entire situation. What would cause a mother to lie about her child?

And yet, when he thought about the short time he'd spent with Rose, his soul overflowed with an odd type of joy, one of liberation. He'd unloaded his fear on Connor, who'd claimed to have the same fear, but Roddy had still been left feeling ashamed. Lesser. Connor had defeated his fear, whereas he was still mired in his. He'd shared all with Rose, and the most wondrous thing of all had happened.

She hadn't judged him.

CHAPTER FOUR

"MAYHAP THEY'LL ALLOW US TO sleep in the stables, Connor. 'Tis nearly midnight and I can smell rain in the air." He slowed his horse, glancing skyward as they drew closer to Sona Abbey.

"I'd say 'tis a most reasonable request. The abbey is supposed to welcome travelers, though I hardly felt welcome on my past visit. I asked about visiting inside, but they were not open to it. Said it was a religious day and no visitors were allowed."

Roddy nodded. "I'm all for trying to spend the night dry." He nodded toward the stables outside the abbey. Two lads were already herding animals inside. Horses didn't like thunder any more than men did. Every thunderstorm reminded him of the day the Grant stable master had been struck by lightning while he was attempting to calm the destriers and get them inside. That had been a somber day indeed. Many of his clan did their best to stay inside during episodes of lightning ever since that fateful day, especially his cousin, Jamie.

Death. It seemed to be waiting for him everywhere these days.

Connor dismounted outside the stables, calling out to the lad just inside. "We'd like to request a night in your stables rather than continue in the approaching storm," he said. As he spoke, an older man, likely the stable master, emerged.

"Och," the man said, clasping his shoulder, "no need for you to sleep here, my lord. We'll have it packed full of

beasts soon. We have a guest house for travelers." He nodded toward Connor's plaid. "Anyone from Clan Grant is
welcome. And you are the only travelers this night. Head
to the kitchens and one of the brothers will share what
we have, likely a smoked fish or a vegetable stew. Mayhap
some bread. Then he'll lead you to the guest house. 'Tis
not protected inside the curtain wall, but I doubt you'll
be bothered this night. A dreadful storm is indeed coming
this way. We'll take good care of your animals, keep them
dry inside."

"Many thanks, my friend," Roddy said.

They hurried along through the gate in the wall because
storm clouds were drifting closer in the moonlight, the
winds blustering while glorious shades of purple and deep
blue danced in the active sky. The first crack of thunder
rang out so they rushed into the kitchens, locating one of
the brothers without a problem.

He introduced himself as Brother Edward. "Here, lads.
Take a trencher of fish stew and an ale with each of you
and head straight to the guest house. The monks tell me
this is to be a mighty thunderstorm. Find your way while
'tis still safe." He placed the food in a basket, which he
handed to Roddy. Connor took up the goblets.

"Our thanks for your hospitality, Brother Edward," Connor said. "My belly has been rumbling for the last hour."

"Eat hearty, lads," he called to them as they turned to
leave. "Follow the path to the right and it will lead you
directly to the guest house." He escorted them to the door
in the curtain wall and pointed them toward the path.

"Not far, I hope," Roddy added as he peered up at the
flashing lights that promised a downpour soon.

Connor added, "Aye, I don't wish to suffer dear Mac's
fate. We are lucky enough to have a building to stay in. I'll
not move again until daybreak."

"If you go through the door in the fence," he said, pointing to it, "you'll find it on the other side of that hedge."

Brother Edward chuckled. "You only need worry about the ghosts."

Connor had been gazing up at the storm, too, but he spun his head to look at the monk. Roddy did the same. Had they heard the man correctly?

"Ghosts?" he repeated.

"Aye, you must know we are not far from a graveyard. One never knows what a storm will blow in." His eyes shone with humor before he turned away.

"Move along, Roddy. 'Tis about to dump on us." Connor shivered as he pushed his cousin toward the door.

They raced toward the door in the fence and made haste to the guesthouse, getting inside just in time. A howling wind and sheets of rain descended on the area almost as soon as they shut the door behind them.

Roddy could swear he heard cackling laughter carried on the wind.

———◆———

Roddy and Connor filled their bellies while they listened to the storm rage all around them. Connor took a swig of ale and said, "Sorry, cousin, this may not have been the best idea."

"Why not?" Roddy glanced around the place, which was clean and well-appointed. "'Tis far better than sleeping on the ground on our plaids. I love sleeping under the stars like our sires did, but not in this weather. I'll take dry ground any day, and I'm sure the horses are much happier in the stable chomping on oats than they'd have been in the thunderstorm. Besides, you wish to explore the abbey, do you not?"

Connor glanced at the torch on the wall, which was flickering wildly from the gusts of wind sneaking in through the small hole in the wooden door. "Right now, I have no interest in leaving this fine guest house. There's water and a garderobe. Four separate rooms attached to the main room and a bottle of wine on the table. I'm not moving." Connor took another bite of his stew. "Mayhap we can break our fast inside tomorrow after the storm moves on. If their morning offerings are as good as this stew, I'm willing to wait, and I'd like you to see the abbess or one of the priests I met before."

"We can surely try. I have a few coins I can donate to their coffers. Mayhap that will get us inside the door."

They finished their meal, talking while the storm raged outside. Then they chose the one room that had two separate beds in case any other travelers arrived seeking shelter. Roddy searched a chest and found a linen square to wash his face and hands, using the full urn on the table. Once he finished all his ablutions, he removed his boots and plopped down on one bed, pleased to see it was a mattress instead of a pallet. "We shall sleep well." He lay on his back, staring up at the ceiling as occasional flashes of lightning lit up the building.

"I'm sure *you* will sleep well. A pair of violet eyes will haunt you." Connor gave him a wry grin as he took to the other mattress, lying with his back against the wall. "Rose is a beauty."

"Aye," Roddy murmured, and as his eyes closed, those violet eyes appeared magically.

The next thing Roddy knew, the loudest clap of thunder he'd ever heard shattered the silence in the guesthouse. He bolted out of bed and leapt to his feet, his hand already reaching for his sword. The he saw *her*, and his hand dropped as quickly as he'd lifted it.

Standing in the doorway was a woman in a billowing gown. He rubbed his eyes to be certain he was seeing clearly, but the vision before him didn't change. This woman, this specter, was transparent.

"Who are you?" he whispered, afraid she would disappear. "*What* are you?"

Her voice was as clear as the ringing of a bell. "You must

come back. You must help her when she arrives." She had red hair and a circle of pearls held the curls in place, the wind threatening to unleash them. Her dress was white with a blue band at the middle and long bell sleeves nearly covering her fingertips. She floated as if buffeted by the storm, her feet not even visible beneath the transparent hem of the gown.

"What? Help whom?" Roddy couldn't believe his own eyes. Was he dreaming, or was there truly some kind of apparition in front of him? One of the shutters blew open with a bang, and lightning lit up the room. He glanced over to see if Connor was awake.

Connor rested on his elbows, staring at the woman in front of them with wide eyes. "A ghost. A real ghost," he muttered.

"You see her, do you not, Connor?" His eyes darted back to the vision in front of them, now flickering in and out as if she was about to leave them. "Connor?" He couldn't look at his cousin anymore, his gaze was once again locked on the vision.

The woman spoke to him once more as she faded away. "She has no one but you." Her hand reached out to touch Roddy before she held her other hand out to Connor. "You must help her."

The specter flickered in front of them like a torch in the wind, the expression on her face as sincere and serious as any he'd ever seen. Could she be real?

"Who are you talking about?" Roddy bellowed at the phantom presence.

She didn't answer.

Connor got to his feet and took one step forward. Another. Reached out a hand toward the spirit.

Roddy had to try one more time. "Who? Who do you want us to help?" he pleaded.

The apparition disappeared as quickly as she'd appeared.

"Are we dreaming?" Roddy whispered, his gaze still

locked on the doorway.

"We must be," Connor said, raking a hand through his hair as if to check that it was intact.

"But you saw her, did you not?"

"Aye, I saw her, but I'll not admit it to anyone. Everyone would think us daft. You must not tell a soul, either. For certes not Brother Edward. Mayhap he conjured her up, or..." Connor disappeared into the central gathering room, only to reappear a moment later shaking his head.

Nothing. The room was empty.

Roddy added, "Or mayhap 'twas a jest. He could have dressed someone up and sent her in here. 'Twas the middle of the night, and the light in here is poor. Mayhap she only appeared ghostly."

Connor considered the suggestion, then shook his head. "Nay, 'twas a spirit. A ghostly presence. I know what I saw, but I'll not tell anyone." His face looked as troubled as if a thousand ghosts stood directly in front of him. "Never."

Neither said anything for a few moments, staring at the door as the storm continued its fury around them, tree branches scraping across the sides of the building in between lightning bolts.

"Roddy?" Connor whispered.

"What is it?" Roddy asked, taking a step back.

"Did you notice she had no feet?"

Roddy peered at his cousin, nodding before asking the question he most dreaded. "Have you any idea who she was she talking about?"

Connor raked his hand through his hair again, tugging on it as if to assure himself he was awake, took a swig of his ale, still on the table between the beds, and paced in a small circle. "I have no idea. Someone who is coming here, I suppose."

For some odd reason, a vision of a dark-haired lass with violet eyes standing on a cliff popped into Roddy's head, but that didn't make sense. Rose lived at MacDole Castle.

She'd have no reason to come to the abbey.

He shook his head to indicate his confusion.

They went back to bed without saying another word, though Roddy had trouble falling back asleep. He dozed off eventually, and when morning came, he was surprised to see Connor already up and seated in a chair against the wall.

"Get dressed. I still want to break our fast." Connor's face was more serious than he'd ever seen it. The vision hadn't left him any more than it had left Roddy.

They gathered their things and followed the path back into the kitchens, in search of the great hall. He had to admit he wasn't very hungry. His belly had churned much of the night.

They located the mother abbess and introduced themselves. She smiled, folding her hands in front of her. "Clan Grant. Aye, you've been most generous in protecting Lochluin Abbey. Many thanks to you. Please break your fast with us. We have porridge and bread for you. 'Twas quite a storm we had last night."

They followed her into the hall.

Connor whispered to Roddy, "I'm getting that bad feeling again about this place."

Roddy asked, "From what? We just came in, and she seems perfectly friendly today."

"True," Connor replied in an undertone. "I cannot explain it, but 'tis there again."

Did it have something to do with the abbess? He'd make sure and ask Connor later if he remembered. There were no monks in sight, but several nuns and a few priests broke bread together. Many of them looked quite young. The abbess turned to them to explain. "We spend much of our time training and educating young people who come to us wishing to become nuns or priests. We do have some monks who keep to themselves in a separate building, and we occasionally have visiting monks, but this main building is used to train our youth. We have many generous benefactors who have bestowed much wealth upon us to help spread the Lord's word throughout Scotland. We send our trained novices out to other abbeys and kirks."

Roddy couldn't think of anything to say, still unable to banish the memory of their ghostly visitor from the night before.

Connor asked, "How many lasses are here, Abbess?"

"Usually a few dozen. Some lads come here wishing to be priests, but we tend to get more young girls." She greeted several people as she led them through the room, weaving around the serving lasses who doted on everyone in attendance.

A priest entered the hall and strode directly to their side. "Who are these men?"

"Father, they are from Clan Grant. They stopped for a place to wait out the storm. As you know, Clan Grant has been verra protective of our sisters and brothers at Lochluin Abbey. I invited them to break their fast before they continue on their journey."

Her smile was broad, but it did not meet her eyes. The undercurrent of hostility between the two was not missed by Roddy.

The priest directed his gaze at them. "Welcome to both of you. We share whatever we have, but we have a verra busy day today so we hope you'll be on your way soon. Warriors can be distracting to our young lasses. We try our best to deliver them from temptation." He spun on his heel and left.

The abbess stopped when they reached a small table where they could be seated alone and away from the others. "If you need anything else, please let me know."

"My thanks, Mother Abbess," Connor said, waiting for her to depart before he took his seat.

As soon as she left, Roddy said, "You were right to be suspicious, and not just because of..." He shrugged. "I've been in Lochluin Abbey many times, but the feeling here is much different."

"This is not a pleasant place," Connor whispered. "But I can't decide why I feel that way."

"Agreed," Roddy whispered back. "Could it be the priest and the abbess? I did sense some dislike there."

"Nay," Connor said. "They may not get along, but there's something else. At Lochluin Abbey, everyone acts happy to be serving God, but I'm not so sure here. 'Tis verra quiet. And I still can't get something else out of my mind."

"The same thing I cannot erase from my mind," Roddy said. After looking all around, making sure he couldn't be overheard, he whispered, "Who are we supposed to help?" He made mention of the ghost without actually saying the word. "Do you suppose she's talking about a lass who is in danger from the Channel of Dubh?"

"I told you never to mention that lass again," Connor ground out.

"No one can hear us." He stopped speaking and held up a hand because a serving lass was headed in their direction.

The lass smiled and did a small curtsy. "My lords, I have porridge for you and a small loaf of bread for you to share. Is there anything else I can get for you?"

Roddy glanced at Connor, who was already shaking his head. "Nay. If Brother Edward is in the kitchens, tell him he made a fine fish stew." He felt he should be complimentary about something. They had been offered generous hospitality. Plus it would give him a chance to speak with the serving lass.

"Brother Edward?" She said, "Aye, if I have the opportunity, I will pass it on."

Roddy wanted to see the lasses who were in residence, thinking perhaps the spirit had spoken of one of them, but there were very few about. "Lass, the abbess said there were over thirty novices here. Where are they all?" Only six sat at a nearby table while three young men sat at a separate table.

"The abbess has sent many of the lasses to the other abbey to clean."

"Other abbey?" Connor asked. "I have not seen another near here."

"Father Seward is having a new abbey built. Abbey of the Angels. We have more students than ever. The lads who wish to be priests and some of the monks are finishing the construction for him."

"A new abbey? Where is it?"

"I have not been there, but 'tis south of here. Less than an hour's journey."

The abbess called out to her. "Ada, please move along." Her tone was a wee bit sharp.

"Aye, Mother Abbess." She smiled and departed, her eyes darting around the hall.

Roddy peered over at Connor. He could see the same exact thought had come to his mind. They had a new place to explore. Mayhap the girl who needed saving was at this new abbey.

CHAPTER FIVE

R OSE HURRIED INTO THE CAVES, ducking into the entrance to the cellars so she wouldn't be seen near the men if the steward or the guard at the gate noticed them returning from the shoreline.

Her mother had strong ideas about lads.

When she arrived in the great hall, her mother was waiting for her, standing with her arms crossed in front of her. "What were you doing with that man out there?" she snapped. "Did you kiss him?"

Rose shook her head, hoping the look of shock she expressed would be enough to hold her mother off. They were alone in the hall, but how she wished someone would interrupt them. Her mother had a way of inspiring a fear in her she hated. Someday she vowed to be strong enough to ignore her mother's eccentricities, but that time had not yet come. Lady MacDole had control over every aspect of her life—she could, and had, make things intolerable for her.

"Don't lie to me! I saw you kissing him on the cliffs. Your poor sire would roll over in his grave if he saw you commit such an act. I'll not stand by while you become a whore. Mark my words. You'll regret this. I think the time has come for you to move on." She spun on her heel and left the hall.

An icy fear crept up Rose's spine because her mother never made empty threats. In fact, she knew there was only one relevant question to ask, if she were able to speak.

Where would her mother send her?

Roddy and Connor headed south, hoping to find the new abbey without any difficulty, but it took three hours longer than they anticipated because it was so well hidden.

Once they were able to ascertain the exact location, they hid their horses in a nearby copse of trees and crept up to the building on foot. The monks had built something just a bit larger than a hut, though it could easily hold four chambers. At present, they were busy building a thatch roof over half the building. The other half was already covered.

The two men crept closer, staying well hidden, hoping to hear comments about the use of the building, but all was quiet. The lasses carried buckets of water in and out of the building, indicating they were involved with cleaning while the men were busy with other tasks. Some worked on the roof, some built pallets and shelves out of wood, but all were busy doing something.

Roddy whispered, "I think they found a deserted hut and added to it. The original building appears older, while the back portion appears to be new."

"And the roof is the same, part old, part new. What the hell do you think this is?" Connor asked. "I doubt the Church of Edinburgh or the bishops are aware of this. The spot is well hidden, so you can surely guess my thoughts."

Roddy nodded, chewing on mint leaves he'd found nearby. "Aye, this is hidden apurpose. Whoever is building this does not want it to be found. And I don't see an altar or a chapel anywhere."

"Exactly. Mayhap they plan on hiding people here for a short time. I fear it's to be used as little more than an inn for traveling lasses."

Roddy met his cousin's eyes, seeing the same fury he felt deep down in his bones. He wished to charge inside and slay everyone involved, yet he knew he couldn't. Besides which, for all they knew, the workers were ignorant of how the place would be put to use. It seemed unlikely they were all directly involved in the Channel of Dubh.

"If we do anything hasty, we'll drive them to another place," Connor said.

"I know. We need to contact Maggie and Will. See what they suggest we do next."

A loud voice interrupted their whispered conversation.

"Hurry up before he comes back. You know what he'll do if we don't have this done."

Connor glanced at Roddy. "Should we wait?"

Roddy shrugged his shoulders. "Would it help? Chances are we'll not know the person."

They didn't have to think on it for long. A man appeared on the other side of the clearing.

They'd never seen him before, but he was English. They knew because he gave one instruction. "Finish the roof today, or you will be flayed alive. We need this ready in a less than a fortnight. He'll be here in a few days, and he may say he needs it in a sennight. Work harder."

Roddy glanced at Connor. "Aye, we need to find Will and Maggie as soon as possible."

Though it hadn't been there original plan, when they left, they bypassed Braden's castle and headed straight for the meeting place for the Band of Cousins, the new hut the group had built near Will's grandfather's cottage.

It was late the next morn when they finally arrived.

Roddy glanced overhead and said, "Seems that Will and Maggie must be here, though the horses are different. I see Will's falcons flying about." Will had trained two falcons, birds of prey he used to scare his enemies. He'd earned the name "The Wild Falconer" because of it.

Maggie and Will, who organized the group's efforts, greeted them warmly at the door. "It's good you're here," Maggie said, ushering them into the main room. "Gavin and Gregor just arrived, and we were about to fill them in on everything we've learned since the Lamont incident."

The Lamont brothers were cruel, unscrupulous men who'd slaughtered Cairstine Muir's family and stolen their keep. Greer Lamont had then claimed Cairstine as his mistress. Braden had killed the bastard and married Cairstine, whom he now lived with in Muir Castle, but the other brother, Blair Lamont, still lived. He'd escaped, and they hoped finding him would help them uncover more of the Channel of Dubh.

Gavin and Gregor, two of the best archers in all the land, joined them as they entered the main room of the house. Roddy was shocked at the progress. The interior looked much more finished than it had on his last visit. Their cousins had kept busy. The main room boasted a new table and chairs, large enough to seat all of the cousins at once, and a huge hearth at the end. The two chambers for sleeping were located at the back, a garderobe attached to the lasses' portion.

Connor let out a whistle. "Gavin, you and Gregor did a fine job with the table and chairs. Didn't know you had such woodworking skills." Indeed, they'd teased the pair on their last visit, for they hadn't thought it possible the work would be done with such precision.

Gavin puffed up with pride as Gregor grinned and checked their work for any scratches.

Maggie said, "Let's chat for a bit. Have a seat."

Everyone settled in around the table and Maggie stood to update her cousins on what she and Will had learned after their most recent trip to Edinburgh. They had gone there while the Grant cousins focused on the coast.

"First, the bad news," Maggie said. "We have been unable to locate Blair Lamont. We hope he'll turn up eventually, but we have no way of knowing whether he's still involved in the Channel. The good news is we've had several other leads. Sources who have heard of lasses being sold in different areas."

Connor raised his hand to interrupt Maggie.

"Aye, Connor?"

"Is there no information on who is leading this entire network? Or are they truly acting individually?"

"From what we've learned there is a coordinator, if you will, of these networks. One who commands a portion of every sale while never even setting eyes upon the lasses or lads. A few of our sources have indicated this person acts mostly out of the Lowlands, possibly as far south as England."

"So if we stop that person, we could stop it all?" Connor asked.

She glanced at Will, nodding for him to answer. "Possibly, but no one seems to know the person by name."

Roddy said, "Mayhap we have information that will help."

Connor leaned forward, resting his arms on the table, and said, "We may have just seen that man. We actually had a successful journey to the west."

"Go ahead, fill us in on what you found." Will waved his hand, indicating they should take over the conversation.

Roddy told them about MacDole Castle sitting atop Loch Linnhe.

"What makes you think they could be involved?" Maggie asked.

Connor took over the explanation. "I saw a long dock on the shoreline, large enough to handle good-sized boats. Roddy met the MacDole lass, and she says she's seen boats in the past, using beacons."

"What else did she tell you? Anything about the cargo or where the boats come from?"

Maggie directed her attention to Roddy. He sighed and said, "Nay. She does not speak. We conversed with her and did our best to communicate, but that was all she could tell us. She only knows that they come in the night and use a beacon."

Connor said, "But the situation is more complicated

than that. There is an abbey not far from there, about an hour. We stopped and spoke with the abbess. She indicated there are usually over thirty lasses there, yet we only saw a handful. One of the serving lasses told us they were all at the new abbey, Abbey of Angels."

"I've never heard of this," Maggie said, looking confused.

"Braden never mentioned it either," Roddy said. "We headed south and located a group working on what appeared to be an abandoned building. The lasses were sprucing up the inside while the lads and monks worked on the roof of a new section just added. Other lads were inside building doors and shelving."

"So, they are expanding a new building that no one knows about." Maggie glanced at Will, then back at Roddy.

"The workers were afraid of getting into trouble if they didn't finish in time. An Englishman appeared out of nowhere, instructing them to finish in less than a fortnight."

Connor added, "Mayhap a sennight."

Will nodded. "An isolated castle, a sea loch with a dock, boats in the night, and a new abbey for young lasses who wish to become nuns. Hmmm. Sounds like a new location for the Channel of Dubh. Mayhap Lamont is involved."

"That's exactly what came to our minds. We thought it best to update you before we investigate further."

They let their words settle as they poured ale for all who were present.

"I think we should all head north," Maggie said at last, "though Will and I will travel to Ramsay land first to inform my father of the situation. Daniel was planning to report back to us tomorrow, so he can join us. In fact, I'll send him off with the two of you, Roddy and Connor. You three can investigate Sona Abbey further and keep watch for any ships in the sea loch, or anything else unusual. I'm going to have Gavin and Gregor search the area, see if anyone else knows about this new abbey."

Daniel Drummond was a new member of the Band of Cousins. Of all of them, he was the best at sneaking and spying, known in jest as the Ghost, so it was a relief they'd have him around to help.

The sound of horses brought their attention to the outdoors. A few moments later, Will's grandfather knocked on the door and stuck his head inside, "William, ye have a visitor."

The door burst open moments later, and Gwyneth Ramsay pushed her way in, Molly behind her.

"Molly?" Maggie said, rushing forward to hug her sister and her adoptive mother. She was clearly as surprised about the visit as the rest of them. "Is something wrong? Why are you here?"

Molly moved inside and sat in an empty chair, holding her head. The gesture sent a wave of foreboding through Roddy. Every Grant and Ramsay knew Molly was a seer. Headaches preceded her premonitions. "Headaches again, Maggie. Bad headaches and I'm worried about you."

Gwyneth said, "I couldn't deter her, stubborn lass. She's convinced something bad is about to happen. Maggie, she's especially worried you may be involved."

Maggie took the chair next to her sister and hugged her lightly. "Molly, you need not worry about me. Mayhap we're about to come upon more trouble, but Will and our cousins will be there to protect me."

Molly teared up, still rubbing the front of her forehead. "I'm glad you are hale. I was so worried. But please be careful. Something nasty is coming. Promise me you'll not take any risks." She gripped her sister's upper arm.

"I promise, Mol. Why don't you lie down? We have mattresses on several pallets. I'll tell Mama everything while you rest." She helped her sister to her feet and led her into one of the adjoining chambers. Their mother followed them and closed the door behind them.

Will's gaze followed the door, concern in his eyes, but

he smiled when he turned back to face them. "I think you all need something in your bellies before you leave, lads. Who's the best cook?"

"I'll make a stew if somebody catches a rabbit or two," Gregor offered.

Connor said, "I'll do the hunting."

Roddy pushed back from the table and said, "I'll see what vegetables I can find to chop up. Will you join me, Gavin?"

Gavin agreed, but not without some grousing about being sent on the less exciting task.

Will headed for the door. "I'll get Grandpapa and have him join us."

They spent the rest of the day strategizing, keeping their conversation pitched low so as not to disturb Molly. They planned their patrols so they wouldn't cross each other's paths, conscious of the Englishman's comment about something happening in a fortnight. All of them were anxious to catch more of the blackguards involved in this Channel.

At dinner, Gregor said, "I cannot ignore the fact that Molly is having headaches. What think all of you about that?"

Roddy glanced at Connor, who glared at him. He didn't have trouble interpreting that look. His cousin wouldn't thank him if he revealed they'd seen a ghost.

Instead, Roddy said, "Have any of you met Paddy the pony? Connor and I can vouch for the fact that he is a bit different than your average Highland pony."

"What exactly do you mean by that?" Gregor asked. "Does he cast spells or something?"

Gavin added, "If so, I need to become friends with him. See if I can convince him to cast a spell on a few lasses."

"You cannot get any on your own, Gavin?" Gregor asked, a wry grin transforming his usually serious face. "But I thought all the lasses liked you better?" he taunted, clearly repeating something Gavin had said.

Gavin ignored him, offering a quick short, "We shall see."

Will said, "I don't ignore unusual gifts from animals, but that probably does not surprise any of you, given my falcons. Remind everyone about Paddy."

Roddy said, "Steenie, five summers old, was lost in the dark and the pony found him. He brought the lad straight to Grant land."

"Steenie probably guided him," Gavin said.

"Impossible. Steenie had never been to Grant land. We still don't know how the two of them found their way in the middle of the night."

The group chewed their food, giving the comment serious thought.

Connor sighed and said, "Anyone who's seen that pony with Steenie knows 'tis an odd relationship. I cannot deny it, no matter how I try."

Gregor said, "A strange pony, Molly having headaches. What's the connection, Roddy?"

Glancing again at Connor, who shot him an even dirtier look, Roddy only said, "I believe Molly, is all. There are strange things in this world, things that cannot be explained."

Connor bolted out of his chair so quickly he knocked it over.

The rest of their time was spent in light banter until they left the following morn.

"Maggie, I hope your sister feels better. For all of our sakes," Roddy said.

Maggie thanked him and wished them luck on their journey. "I'll send Daniel along as soon as he arrives." She returned to her sister's bedside, leaving the travelers alone.

"Godspeed to you," Gavin said to Roddy and Connor, waving once he and Gregor had mounted.

"And to you," Roddy said, saying a silent prayer for God's help, too.

He had two things on his mind—a lovely lass with violet eyes, and a ghost who'd come to them in the night and told them to help a lass.

He had a sinking suspicion both had something to do with the Channel of Dubh.

———————

The day after Rose shared a kiss with Roddy, her mother brought her to the abbey. Her mother had barely spoken to her at all since confronting her in the great hall. Rose did her best not to dwell on the thought that she was being sent to a different prison. Despite her mother's threat, there remained a slim possibility they were attending the abbey for religious reasons or for her mother to make a donation to the abbey.

Sona meant joyous in Gaelic, but what was joyous about a church full of nuns and monks? There were no cliffs or pounding waves there, none of the rough, rugged beauty she loved at home. She'd been eager for something more, aye, but she knew she'd not find it here. Thoughts of the warm lips of a warrior in red plaid were foremost in her mind.

Once they arrived, the stable master sent for two nuns to escort them into the abbey. The abbess met them at the door, and the two other nuns peeled away. The abbess was a short, rotund woman with fair skin that stood out against her dark robes. Rose had the sense the woman was quite strict, but she didn't seem unkind. She wore a smile that did not reach her eyes, though the tiny lines at the edges seemed to deepen. Her presence filled the small foyer they stood in, empty other than a narrow bench and table.

"Mother Marion, I'm so pleased to see you again. This is my lovely daughter, Rose. I've mentioned her to you before." Her mother always referred to the mother abbess as Mother Marion.

"Aye, good day to you, my dear." She stood as straight

as an arrow, her hands folded in front of her and hidden inside the bell sleeves of her robe.

"Please remember that my daughter cannot hear or speak." Her mother's chin lifted a bit as though she wished to challenge the abbess. Was this to be a battle of wills of some sort? Her mother was quite controlling, but she guessed the abbess was accustomed to being in control, especially here.

"I do recall that, Lady MacDole, but I do not wish to treat her as though she doesn't exist." She smiled directly at Rose again.

She had a sudden urge to hug the abbess. Most people tended to ignore her once they learned she couldn't hear or speak. Mayhap that was her mother's reason for telling the lie. If her mother did leave her here, at least she'd be around other people. Anyone would be better company than her mother, even the mother abbess.

Lady MacDole sighed and folded her hands in front of her, mimicking the abbess. "Your consideration for her feelings is commendable, Mother Marion, but I know her best. She often becomes anxious if she doesn't understand what others are saying to her. That is exactly the reason I have kept her secluded at home of late. It would be too troublesome for her to be around others where she cannot communicate."

"Perhaps we could teach her to read," Mother Marion said as she led them down the passageway and up the stairs to the chambers for the lasses who were to be novices in the nunnery. "While we do not usually instruct our students in reading, perhaps an exception could be made in Rose's case due to the unusual circumstances."

Rose knew how her mother would respond to that suggestion. Rather than listen, she directed her attention to her surroundings. The passageway was well lit with candles in sconces, the ornate shape adding a regal feeling to the surroundings that seemed out of place.

How long would she be expected to stay here?

Her mother's voice, presently a pleasant lilt, broke into her awareness, "Her dear sire attempted to teach her, but he was unsuccessful. There's no reason to waste anyone's time on lessons. Come along, dearest." She ushered her daughter in front of her as they followed the abbess through the network of passageways.

Rose wished she could speak, because if she could, she would shout loud enough for every nun and monk inside the abbey to hear her declare that she wanted to learn how to read. That nothing would please her more, that she would work harder than any student they'd ever seen if someone would just take the time to teach her.

They passed the open double doors to the great hall, and she peered inside, hoping to see others her own age.

Rows of trestle tables filled the halls, but they were empty. As they neared the staircase at the end of the passageway, singing voices rang out from the chapel. She steeled herself not to respond to the beautiful sound echoing down the passageway. Her mother clucked her tongue, but the abbess only quirked her brow. "We sing to the Lord."

The abbess stopped, paused, then pivoted on her heel to face Lady MacDole. "Heavens above, how will we be able to get her to say her vows when the time comes?"

Rose nearly stopped in her tracks at this pronouncement, but she forced herself to continue, casting a sideways glance at her mother.

Her mother's threat from the other night popped into her mind again.

You'll regret this. I think the time has come for you to move on.

So, *this* was what she'd had in mind. She would force her to become a nun.

Rose's mother didn't even flinch. "You'll have plenty of time before you need worry about that. She can do basic signs to indicate what she needs. For instance, food or drinks, or if she is cold, she'll shiver for you. I'm sure you get the idea." Those last sentences were delivered with a bite. Sometimes, Rose wondered if her mother would prefer it if she'd just freeze to death out on the cliffs.

The abbess reached over and patted Rose's shoulder. "I'm sure she'll get along well here. I'll introduce her to the other novices at the evening meal. The two of you must be tired after your long journey. Perhaps you would like to rest for a bit. I'll have one of the maids assist her with her trunk. She'll be staying in this chamber," she added, indicating an open door off to the left.

The chamber was small and chilly with no hearth in sight. There were two pallets on opposite walls, a plaid and a fur folded on the end of each, and there was a large gold cross on the far wall. A table with two chairs sat underneath the cross. Her trunk would sit at the end of one bed, but beyond that, there was very little room.

Her mother said, "No need for anyone to attend to me. I'll be on my way, as I wish to return before dark. I'll just say my goodbyes and leave. If you'll summon the maid to have her trunk brought up, they can quickly arrange her chamber for her."

The abbess gave a slight bow and headed back through the passageway toward the stairway. The poor woman started to say, "Rose, if you are in need…" She stopped mid-sentence, apparently thinking better of speaking to a supposedly deaf woman.

"I'll give my darling girl one last hug before I leave." Lady MacDole waved as the abbess descended the staircase. Rose wished to grab the woman's arm and reel her back, but she knew better. She knew her mother.

As soon as the abbess was out of hearing range, Rose's mother gripped her arm and shoved her into the chamber. "Now, you will remain here until the Lord has forgiven you for your transgressions. You must beg His forgiveness, or I'll be forced to have you take your vows and remain here as a nun for the rest of your days. Think on that and decide what you will do."

Rose nodded, the same way she always did with her mother. If she were not agreeable, she'd be punished accordingly. As much as she wished to reveal her secret to the mother abbess and petition her for help, her mother was a frequent visitor to the abbey. If Rose were to reveal her secret, this would not be the best place. Her mother would know before the day was out. Of that much she was certain since she visited both Father Seward and the mother abbess frequently. Nay, she would have to continue the pretense of being deaf, at least for the time being.

"Remember," her mother said, "it is your fault you bleed every month. Shame on you for causing it with your disgraceful sins. Until it ceases, you'll remain here."

She dropped her hand as if glad to be rid of her and departed without another word.

Rose's eyes misted as she sat on the pallet in this small, stuffy room where the one person left in her family had abandoned her. While she would never take her own life, she did often wish she were dead. It would be much easier.

CHAPTER SIX

———◆———

W HEN RODDY AND CONNOR ARRIVED at Muir Castle, they informed Braden of all that had transpired, including their meeting with the Band of Cousins. Braden asked, "I still don't understand why you returned to MacDole Castle. What made you suspect something underhanded?"

Connor just arched his brow and grinned, turning toward Roddy and giving him the chance to answer.

Roddy couldn't deny the truth of the matter. "I met a dark-haired lass who caught my interest. We met on the cliffs, but I frightened her. I became more intrigued with her when I saw her inside the castle."

"Just because of her beauty? Is that why Connor is guffawing?"

"Nay, not just because of that, though she is quite bonnie. Her mother told me she couldn't speak or hear, but I sensed it wasn't the complete truth. Besides, Connor hadn't uncovered anything at all, so I wished to go back. The castle is directly on the sea loch, which seemed like a possible loading point for the Channel. Connor agreed with me."

"About the lass?" Braden teased him.

"Nay, you fool. But speaking of the lass, when I returned, she explained to me that she can indeed hear, but she cannot speak. So, you see, I was right."

Connor chided, "We were both right. Both of us suspected something strange was afoot at MacDole Castle. If the Channel is active in the area, they must know something. Maggie and Will agree, so we're going back."

Braden asked, "Why did she lie about not being able to hear?

"'Tis her mother who insists on the lie, although I have yet to determine why. I managed to get Rose alone and she explained the truth to me. We do have trouble communicating, but 'tis much easier now that I know she can hear my words. Lady MacDole is a strange woman. She keeps herself isolated from everyone and everything. She'll not give us any information at all. I wish to speak with the household help." Then he grinned at Connor. "And if I happen to see a beauty with violet eyes along the way, then so be it."

What he didn't say was that a new dream had haunted his sleep, much more pleasant than his nightmares of the water. Rose spoke to him in the dream, and her voice was the sweetest sound he'd ever heard. He always awoke feeling the urgent need to see her.

Clearing his throat, he told Braden the rest of it. The strangeness they'd sensed at Sona Abbey. The new abbey they'd seen. The Englishman who'd overseen the work.

"What's your plan now?" Braden asked.

"After we return to MacDole Castle to talk to the help, mayhap ask Rose a few more questions, we'll travel to the abbey to see if we can find anything else out about the new abbey. We have about a fortnight to figure out what they have planned."

Braden scratched his head. "'Tis strange indeed. We haven't heard anything about a new abbey, even from the stable master. You're hoping not to attract notice, so I'd best stay back, but if anything changes, I'd be happy to join you."

"If Daniel shows up, send him in our direction. We'll stay the night if you do not mind, then head out on the morrow."

They left the next morning at dawn.

When they finally arrived at the castle, they were surprised to find Lady MacDole outside the curtain wall chatting with her steward. As soon as she caught sight of them, she stalked straight over, coming to a stop beside Roddy's horse. "Lad, I know why you're here. Remove it from your mind. My daughter is no longer here. She's to take her vows as a nun. I've just delivered her to the abbey, and she'll not be allowed visitors for a long time."

Roddy's jaw dropped open. Her words stunned him. It didn't take long before the news brought back that transparent specter from a few nights before.

You must come back. You must help her when she arrives.

Fortunately, Connor jumped right into the conversation. "We are not here for that reason. When we were last here, we asked you if you'd seen any strange ships in the loch. We've received an update of such importance that we felt the need to return. We've received word young lassies are being stolen and shipped off from a base along the water. The location of your castle gives us hope that mayhap someone has witnessed something. A lone ship in the night, strange sounds coming from the ocean, anything at all. We'd hoped to interview your staff, see if they could be of assistance."

"You may speak with the stable lads and my steward, but that's as far as you'll get. I'll not have my serving maid fretting over being sent away on a boat. Your suggestion that we might have any knowledge of such a thing is preposterous. I have never heard a single rumor about it. You have one hour, then be gone." She spun on her heel, lifted her chin, and stomped off as though they were the worst offenders she'd ever met.

Roddy raised his eyebrows and looked at Connor. "Now, do you understand why I wished to come here?"

Connor merely replied, "I'll take the steward, you head to the stable lads."

The stable lads were quite young, probably around ten or eleven summers. "Greetings to you both," Roddy said.

"Are you the only two lads who handle the horses?"

"Aye," the taller of the two replied. "Our sire is the stable master, but when he has other duties, we help out."

"Where do you live?"

"Over yonder. Our hut is north of the cliffs."

"Are you near the loch? Do you go there often?"

They both shook their heads. "We don't live on the water, but we do go fishing in the summer." He could tell they hadn't met many warriors, for their attention was more focused on his weaponry than his face.

"Have you heard about any ships traveling in the night?"

They both shook their heads in unison again. "My lord, may we ask you a question?" the youngest one asked, peering at his brother first.

"Aye. Ask away."

"Where did you get a sword that size? I've not seen one that big before," the lad asked.

"I'm a warrior for Clan Grant. My sire had this one made for me."

"What must we do to earn one?" the older one asked, leaning forward as if telling a secret.

Roddy leaned forward also. "You have to be honorable, trustworthy, and a hard worker. Then, if you fight for Clan Grant, you'll get your own weapon from the armory." He winked and left the lads, wandering about a bit before he left. He followed the path down to the loch, but nothing had been disturbed since his last visit. No footprints, refuse, or anything else to indicate someone else had been there.

When Roddy met up with Connor at the front gate an hour later, neither of them had any more information than when they'd arrived.

They reclaimed their horses and rode for a while without speaking.

"What now?" Connor finally asked.

"I'm heading to the abbey to ask about Rose. I still don't like any of this." Roddy glanced around the property, wondering if they could believe anything they'd been told. "I sense the stable lads don't know much, but why do I feel that the rest are lying? I don't believe they haven't seen anything in those waters. We know it's happening, so why wouldn't they know about it?"

"I agree. The steward is lying. I haven't decided about Lady MacDole, but I'm certain he knows more than he's saying."

"I need to speak with Rose," Roddy said.

"But Lady MacDole said you won't be allowed to see her," Connor reminded him.

Roddy snorted. "And you think that will stop me?"

———◆———

Rose had slept very little because she was in a strange place. Without the waves crashing outside her window, it was eerily and uncomfortably quiet. She didn't like it.

It struck her that this was how her daily life would be if she were deaf in truth. How she wished she could confide in the mother abbess, but she did not wish to anger her mother. She'd seen her mother's ire in the past. She did not relish the idea of seeing it again.

A memory tickled in the back of Rose's mind, asking to be released, but she forced herself not to think on it as she dressed in a dark blue wool gown. She headed down the stairs toward the hall, hoping she could at least find something to break her fast with soon. Did the others know she couldn't speak? Would the abbess help her?

She'd taken no more than ten steps before a lass down the passageway hurried toward her. "Greetings. Are you new here? My name is Constance. Shall we go down to the great hall together?"

Constance had a beautiful mop of red curls and a smile that would light up any chamber. Rose's first instinct was to trust her, so she waited for the lass to come to her. Worried she wouldn't be able to communicate, she pasted a smile on her face and tried to think of what to do next. To her surprise, she didn't need to do anything—Constance took her hand and tugged her along behind her, leading through the passageways and then down the staircase toward the great hall.

Constance turned again and said, "Are you a guest or are you going to take your vows? I'm not sure yet if I will or not. I haven't decided. My mother didn't want me at home any longer because I have seven brothers and sisters. But I like it better here. I can read as many books as I like, and they have so many! I learned from my brother, though my mother never found out about it. She wouldn't have allowed me to learn to read because I'm a lass. How about you? Do you read?" She promptly wrinkled her nose and said, "You did not tell me your name yet."

They were just outside the great hall, but it would be best to get this out sooner rather than later. Rose did the best she could to let Constance know of her failings. She hated that word, but her mother had always referred to her inability to speak as a failing.

Covering her ears and shaking her head, she tried to indicate to Constance that she could not hear. Then she covered her mouth with her hand and shook her head.

"What? You cannot eat? You cannot hear me? Oh my, that would be a definite problem."

One of the nuns came along briskly and set her hands on Rose's shoulders. "Constance, this is Rose. She has just joined us. The abbess says she cannot hear or speak. Will you show her where to get her porridge, please?"

Constance's face jumped from one emotion to the next—pity, hope, sadness, then excitement. The sweet girl would never be able to hide her feelings, which Rose considered a great quality to have in a friend.

A friend. Something she'd always dreamed of having someday. Though she loved her castle in the sky, as she'd always thought of it when she was a young lass, her father had often lamented that it kept her from having friends. Would Constance be her first true friend?

She prayed it would be so. If she had just one friend, someone she could trust, she could share so much more of herself.

Not yet. She took a deep breath and reminded herself she must be patient.

Constance tucked Rose's hand against her side and led the way into the hall. She babbled all the way, much to Rose's delight. Her world was no longer silent.

When she entered the hall, she almost stopped to stare at everything in awe. It was much larger than the Mac-Dole hall. Rows and rows of trestle tables were arranged on the stone floor. Many crosses hung on the walls, but only a few tapestries, mostly of saints. Constance's voice echoed because the chamber was far from full, though other young lasses were moving about and chatting quietly. A large hearth sat on either end of the hall, blazing fires heating up the cold stone walls.

Constance whirled around to speak with her again. "I'll show you everything. I've never known anyone who couldn't hear or speak. What a terrible life for you. You're quite beautiful, you know. If there were lads here, they'd be chasing you everywhere. Straight black hair is far more appealing than my messy red curls. The nuns are always after me to tie it back, but it just won't go. Your hair will be lovely in a bun just so atop your head." They took a few more steps toward the serving table at the side of the hall. Utensils, bowls, and goblets sat at one end, and a huge pot of porridge sat on the other.

Constance's jaw suddenly dropped as if she'd thought of something important. She spun around to face Rose, a wide grin on her face. "I've a wondrous idea. I'm a verra good at drawing, so mayhap I can help you communicate like that. Though 'twill be difficult to get the utensils I need." As they reached the side table, she held up her hand as if she had a writing utensil in it, and asked, "Can you draw? Can you read? If not, I could teach you! But I'd have to see if the nuns will give me the necessary tools. Though I could show you the letters in the books from the library. We are allowed one book at a time, and there are many picture books."

Because of her mother's insistence that she not be allowed to read, Rose had taken the liberty of hiding a few of her sire's favorite books in her chamber. Afraid to bring them along to the abbey, she'd hidden them under her bed before leaving the castle, knowing her mother would probably never step inside her chamber.

Constance seemed excited about the prospect of teaching her, something Rose wanted almost as much as she wished to see Roddy Grant again. She'd had a dream about the handsome warrior last night, but this time it was different. They'd both been talking, sharing their thoughts. It had been as lovely as any dream she'd ever had.

Thoughts of Roddy Grant gave her more courage. Would she dare to defy her mother in this setting?

She shook her head to answer Constance's question, indicating she could neither draw nor read.

To her surprise, Constance wrapped her arms around her and squeezed her until the breath nearly left her lungs. "Do not worry. I will help you. I'll make sure the mean lasses stay away, and only the kind lasses become your friends. I'll tell you exactly everything you must do."

Rose couldn't help but focus on two words.

Mean lasses?

They sat together and Constance indicated for Rose to stay seated while she fetched something else from the side table. When she returned with a bit of honey, Rose nodded her thanks to Constance, who continued to babble. "I think we could come up with signs to indicate certain things. Why don't you put your hands together like this—" she held her palms flat against each other as though in prayer, "—then you could nod. That would mean thank you and you're welcome."

They both did the small bow over their hands, and Constance broke into delighted giggles.

"I'll teach you to read and write, then you can write your messages to me." She giggled again and whispered, "We'll have our own secret signs." Constance winked and pointed from Rose's chest to her own. "Secrets. Friends."

Rose struggled not to shed tears. When had anyone other than her sire offered to help her? Her mother spent as little time as possible with her. Her aunt, the wife of her sire's brother, had visited many times prior to his death, but she hadn't visited since his passing. If she had to guess, her mother had suggested they needed time alone. She'd heard her tell others the same, guaranteeing their isolation. *Her* isolation. There were no young people in her life, and until now, the only place she'd ever encountered any lasses or wee laddies had been at the kirk.

Was her life about to change for the better?

If so, she'd never go home.

Rose was fine.

Her mother would not hurt her own child.

Perhaps she wished to become a nun.

Roddy kept repeating the thoughts, he still did not believe them. None of them rang true for him. He had a sick feeling in his gut, something that twisted one way and then the other, no matter how he tried to reason with himself.

His sire and Uncle Alex always swore by their hunches...

As they approached the abbey, Connor turned to him and said, "I'll wait out here for you once you go inside."

"Why not come with me?"

"If something is going on, they're unlikely to come out and tell us. I'll find my way back to the stables and listen to all that's going on." He paused for a moment, then said, "And I'm *not* going back into that other building."

"So you'll listen like Uncle Logan would?"

A wry grin crossed Connor's face at the mention of the uncle they all strived to emulate. Logan Ramsay, Maggie and Gavin's father, worked as a spy for the Scottish Crown. There was only one person who could soften his edge— his wife, Gwyneth. Uncle Logan adored her.

"Nay, Uncle Logan isn't who I was thinking about exactly, but you're close." Connor dismounted a short distance outside the abbey, handing his favorite horse an apple as he patted his withers.

"What's on your mind, then?" Roddy asked once he'd dismounted, standing with his hands on his hips.

"I was thinking about Aunt Gwyneth. Remember the stories about how she and Uncle Logan met? Wasn't she almost sold across the waters? She fought off one of her captors and gained a reputation for going after a man's bollocks. I was wondering what kind of network there was back then. That was decades ago." Connor reached down for a blade of grass, carefully choosing the right one before placing it in the corner of his mouth.

How the hell had he recalled that? "You're right. I do remember hearing that. Didn't she threaten to cut off Uncle Logan's bollocks?"

Connor broke into a wide grin, his white teeth nearly glowing. "How I wish I'd been a witness to that."

They laughed together, then Roddy asked, "What made you think of Aunt Gwyneth?"

Connor stared up at the sky as dusk approached. "Most lasses aren't trained to fight. If the Channel captures Rose, do you think she'll be able to fight to protect herself?"

Roddy refused to dwell on the worst possible outcome. "I haven't known the lass long, but I sense a powerful will in her. Aye, she'd be strong enough to fight back, but I doubt she knows how to use a dagger. 'Tis something she

must learn if she doesn't have that skill. Just in case…"
Roddy stared at the ground and covered his face with his
hands. "I'll teach Rose how to protect herself."

They arrived at the stables, and two lads came out to
assist them. Once the lads took their horses, they found
their way to the main gates, different from the approach
they'd taken the other night.

"State your business," the guard shouted as he approached.

"I'm here to visit Rose MacDole, if you please."

"There's no Rose MacDole here. Take your leave."

While the stable master had greeted them kindly just a
few days before, this guard was as brusque as could be. He
doubted he'd get much information from the man. It was
obvious he wouldn't get a welcome this time.

"She's new. Her mother told me she's here. She's considering taking her vows."

"I said no Rose MacDole. Leave now. Unless you are
looking to spend the night in our guest house, you are not
welcome." The man's hand moved to the hilt of his sword.

Connor cast him a quick glance to let him know he
would not be spending another night in the ghost house,
as he had referred to it the other day. Then he headed back
toward the stables.

A fury begged to be let loose, but Roddy maintained a
calm exterior while his insides churned. He forced himself to take in all the details of the abbey, just in case he
needed to make a desperate move. It was a plain abbey, not
as ornate as Lochluin Abbey, but the area was well fortified
and there were plenty of guards about. One would not
sneak away from Sona Abbey easily or get inside without
some skills.

Other than a ghost, Roddy thought, which made him
think of their cousin. He couldn't wait to see Daniel to let
him know they'd seen a real ghost. Where the hell was he?

"You're sure about that?" he pressed. "She likely arrived
yesterday." His gaze continued to scan the area, but there

was no sign of Rose—and no sign of anyone who might have a kinder greeting for him.

"No Rose. Leave now. No visitors are allowed on certain days. This is one of them."

Another peculiarity, to be sure.

He turned to take his leave, but a soft giggle caught his attention. He glanced over his shoulder and saw two lasses peeking through a small area at the entrance. They were partly concealed by the thick hedge. He'd hoped one would be dark-haired, but one was blonde and the other had hair the color of chestnuts.

"I'll be your rose, warrior." The brown-haired lass licked her lips and parted them with a sigh.

Roddy pivoted without giving her another look. The guard watched him, so he continued to move, wondering why the lasses were allowed so close to the front gate.

He doubted the mother abbess was aware her students were flirting with a stranger.

When he arrived back at the stables next to Connor, he silently retrieved his horse, interrupting the animal's snack on the long green grasses. He got a snort for his rudeness, which he ignored as he mounted.

"Leaving so soon?" Connor asked. "I haven't even had time to listen to anyone in the stables."

"They're lying. Said she's not here. The guards at the gate are much different than anyone we encountered the other day."

Connor mounted and followed behind him. "Will you tell me what happened, or are you too angry right now?"

Once they were a ways down the path, Roddy said, "Let's make our way to Muir Castle and hope Braden has heard something. I will pursue this further, but not without reinforcements."

"Your temper is flaring, aye?"

"Aye. I don't know where Rose is, but I'll find her."

Out of nowhere, an owl swooped down in front of him,

nearly spooking his horse into rearing back. He watched as the bird landed on a nearby tree and then turned to face him, its golden eyes pinning him to his spot.

He swore the creature stared straight at him, its piercing eyes causing Roddy's heart to pound for a few moments before he pulled his gaze away and continued on their journey.

He wouldn't be distracted by an odd fowl, no matter how rare it was to see owls in the daytime.

He had to find Rose.

CHAPTER SEVEN

R OSE SAT AT A DESK in a small chamber outside the
library, Constance at her side. Rose had been here for
several days, and she already knew Constance would be
her friend for life. In fact, she debated telling her the truth
about her hearing.

She chewed on her lower lip as she studied the letters
on the page in the large book in front of her. Her sire had
taught her all of the letters, but she didn't comprehend
how they could be put together to make words.

Constance had searched for quite a while before she
found a picture book to illustrate some basic words. She'd
started with simple ones. Lass, lad, bed, cat, dog. These were
words Rose remembered from her long-ago lessons with
her father.

Her new friend reviewed the list again. "This one is
mother, you see it starts with the letter M."

Rose traced the M with her fingertip, then did the same
with the other letters in the word. She'd practiced on her
own after her sire's death, usually late at night when she
knew her mother would not catch her.

"Now you try. Can you read these words?"

Demonstrating an admirable degree of wisdom, Constance moved on to other words that might be useful to
Rose: good and bad, father and abbess, God, hungry, hurt,
love, and help me.

How she admired her friend.

Constance had already done so much to help her communicate. Guilt weighed down on her shoulders, but the

guilt wasn't what made her tell the truth—it was the desire to reveal herself fully to her friend. Using some of the signs they'd agree upon, she did her best to communicate to Constance that she could hear but not speak.

"Truly?" Constance clapped her hands, cheered, and then wrapped her in a hug so tight it hurt.

Rose grinned but held her finger to her lip to shush Constance. Then she mouthed the word "secret," and turned to the picture for "mother."

"I'll keep your secret, Rose. 'Tis your mother who makes you lie? Is that what you are trying to tell me?"

She nodded, but as soon as she saw the pained expression on her friend's face, she almost regretted telling her. Constance was a softhearted person. Rose reached out and squeezed her hand, encouraging her to continue.

Her friend nodded, but before she returned to the lesson, she whispered, "I know I'm supposed to be kind to all, especially in the house of the Lord, but I don't think I like your mother verra much."

The lessons continued at a much quicker pace once Constance knew Rose could hear her. She'd already learned so much more than she'd ever hoped.

When their lesson came to an end, Constance said, "I love when your eyes light up so. They are such a beautiful color and they turn lavender when you are pleased with your work."

That night at dinner, two new lasses came to eat with them: Ada and Euphemie. Ada appeared to be pleasant and willing to make friends, but Euphemie harbored an undercurrent of anger about everything. Her brown hair seemed to darken with her changing mood.

"Your name is Rose?" Euphemie said. "Do you have a lad who likes you, Rose? We saw someone at the gates the other day looking for a lass named Rose. His hair was like spun gold and his skin was golden bronze from the sun. Do you know him, lass?"

Rose didn't answer because she couldn't. She struggled to contain her excitement upon discovering that Roddy Grant had come to see her. Why hadn't he been allowed in? She'd been here two days ago. She couldn't let on that she'd understood Euphemie's words, so she used her passive face to stare at the new girl.

"Are you going to answer me?" Euphemie pursed her lips and tipped her head as she waited, her gaze narrowing to slits.

Constance said, "Euphemie, she cannot hear or speak. Leave her be, please."

Euphemie got a strange look on her face, then her eyes lit up and she quirked her brow at them. "Are you daft then? Anyone who cannot talk must be daft. Why would a lad as handsome as that come looking for a daft girl?"

"Euphemie!" The shout rang out across the hall.

"Aye, Sister Murreall?" The lass bolted out of her seat, assuming the look of a penitent—hands clasped together, head bowed.

"You will not tease the new lass. Do you understand me?" Sister Murreall strode over to stand in front of Euphemie while Ada stood behind her, peeking over her shoulder. "The same applies to you, Ada. You will not tease someone who has failings the rest of us do not. Be grateful 'tis not you who cannot hear or speak."

"Aye, Sister. Please do forgive me." The words didn't match Euphemie's posture. She looked rigid with anger, even more so the longer the nun stood in front of her, and no wonder—the woman of the cloth was chastising her in front of the entire hall.

The nun's finger came out of her bell sleeve and pointed toward Rose. "You will apologize now."

Euphemie turned to face Rose with a hateful expression. The voice came out as sweet as honey, but the look in her eyes showed her true feelings. "My apologies to you, Rose."

Sister Murreall said, "You will come with me, please." She pivoted and headed out of the hall.

Euphemie leaned close to Rose. "I hope you can look at my lips and know what I'm saying because this message is meant just for you." She poked her in the chest and said, "This is all. Your. Fault. You will pay for it."

Ada followed her out of the hall, but she shrugged as she went, as if to apologize for her friend.

Rose stared after the departing lasses, wondering what to make of the situation.

Constance took Rose's hand in hers, cocooning it as she patted it. "Do not worry. She likes to talk nasty, but she rarely carries out her promises. Let's keep working on your reading tonight. Just forget about Euphemie."

How she hoped she could.

———◆———

Roddy and Connor had spent the last couple of days searching the area, hoping for some other clues about the new abbey, the MacDoles, or any boats in the sea loch, but they had not met with any success. They were approaching Braden's castle near dusk on a narrow path in the forest when a grunting sound reached Roddy's ears. He spun his head around to look at Connor. "Did you just hear a boar?"

Out of the bushes ahead of them came four wild pigs, snorting and grunting as they charged toward them at a fierce pace. Roddy pulled his bow out, set up his arrow, and let it fly, taking out the largest of the beasts. Connor hit another, but then one of the remaining two began to run in a circle and bumped into Roddy's horse. The beast promptly reared, unseating Roddy. He landed on his back in the middle of a small clearing.

One of the boars headed straight toward him.

He froze.

Connor's shouts pulled him out of his trance. "Roddy,

grab your sword or he'll kill you!"

Sweat broke out across Roddy's forehead, covered the palm of his hand. He finally reached for the hilt of his sword, but his hand was not moving nearly fast enough. He was certain he was about to die. All he could do was stare as the two beasts headed straight toward him.

"Roddy!"

Connor's voice echoed across the clearing as he raced toward him, taking one of the boars out with his sword.

The remaining boar was almost upon Roddy when something finally triggered his reactions and he pulled out his sword, swinging it in a wide arc and hitting the remaining pig with such a force that he not only sliced it open, but sent it flying through the air, landing in a bloody heap on the other side of the clearing.

"Son of a bitch, Roddy. I didn't think you'd ever draw your weapon. What the hell happened? I've never seen you like that." Connor cleaned and sheathed his weapon, then hurried over to his side, gripping his shoulder and shaking him a bit as he continued to stare into the bushes. "Roddy? Are you hale?"

He finally dropped his weapon to the ground, then picked it up to clean it before resheathing it. Pacing a small circle, he stared at Connor. "I don't know what happened. I froze. I know not why. I..." What else could he say? The thing he'd long feared had finally happened. He was so afraid of dying that his fear had paralyzed him.

His days as a warrior were done. Who would wish to take him along in battle when he couldn't be certain he would draw his weapon?

To Rose's delight, Sister Murreall had moved Constance into her chamber, but her friend had become ill with cramps the very next night. She'd gone to the infirmary, and Rose was on her own the following morning.

She could do this. She dressed carefully in the dark gray wool gown supplied by the abbey for their students. As soon as she descended the stairs, Euphemie came over to greet her, then leaned down and quietly whispered, "Still daft, are you? Ugly and stupid. I'll bet I can get you to do something that will get you in trouble, and you'll never suspect a thing until you're in Father Seward's office and he has the switch in his hand. No one will save you then. Not even your friend Constance." The gleam in her eye told Rose how much she enjoyed taunting people.

Rose ignored her, pretending that she could neither hear nor understand Euphemie's words. The mean lass found a seat at the end of the same trestle table, but Rose was happy to ignore her. There was a certain pleasure in knowing that, unbeknownst to Euphemie, she understood every harsh word the lass had said.

She'd be watching Euphemie.

Midway through the meal, Rose decided to add honey to her porridge, so she got up from her seat and went to the side table where the flavorings were kept.

A tittering started behind her, but she ignored it, finishing her task before she returned to the table. Then she was forced to turn toward the tittering. Euphemie was standing by Rose's empty chair, pointing to the seat, now stained with blood.

"See? She is a fool. She does not even know when she bleeds." Euphemie's voice carried to the others and the laughter grew louder. Rose wished to cover her ears, but that would give her lie away, so she didn't. Instead, she dropped her bowl on the table and raced back to her room, horrified that she'd bled all over.

She would surely die of embarrassment. Did Euphemie know that women bled when they were being punished? She desperately needed to speak with Constance. Well, not speak, but be near her. She needed the confidence her dear friend exuded, the comfort she offered her.

As soon as she was alone in her chamber, she disrobed and found rags to stuff between her legs before donning a new gown. After she tossed the bloody clothing on the floor, she fell onto the bed sobbing.

She sobbed for most of the morning, her thoughts full of the other girls' laughter and Euphemie's cruel face. When she finally was able to force the scene from her mind, her mother's voice replaced it.

"God is punishing you for what you did. I saw you kissing that boy. Lasses do not kiss boys until they are married, and now he will force you to pay. You will bleed every month until God feels you have mended your ways. Women do not cavort with rogues but stay at home until their sire marries them off properly. You must pray every night until the Lord forgives your sinful ways. And if I ever see you kiss another boy, I will lock you up for a month. Do you hear me? A month!"

Rose had tried to be good, but every month she bled, and every month her mother would come in and chastise her for her sinful, dirty ways.

And then she'd caught her kissing Roddy, which had made everything so much worse. To her mother's mind, the only way out of her predicament was for her to beg forgiveness at the abbey.

And now all the lasses in the abbey knew about her sinful behavior. How could she ever hold her head high again?

She cried and cried until she fell asleep.

It was almost dark when she awakened. She lay there thinking about all that had transpired, wishing that Constance were there with her. Her friend would know what to do.

Instead, the door opened and a man's face appeared in the crack. It was Father Bernard Seward. "Rose," he whispered. "You must get up and eat something. I heard about your troubles. I'm sending you to the infirmary. They'll help you with your female issues."

She sat up and stared at him, wondering if he meant

what he'd said. His kindness was unexpected, though she did not know him well.

"Can you walk? I'll go with you. You may spend the night there. I do not want you alone in here." She told him with her actions what she couldn't tell him with her words. She stood and followed him out of the room and toward the stairs. The infirmary was on the floor above them at the end of the north passageway. Father Seward led the way, and she was glad to follow. When they arrived, he spoke with the nun in a voice too soft for her to hear. Then he patted her shoulder, smiled at her, and left.

To her delight, the nun led her into a small room with two beds in it, and Constance was in the other bed. The nun pointed to the bed and gave her a pile of fresh rags to use. She blushed because the nun was obviously aware of her shameful secret.

She hadn't known kissing a boy was sinful. They'd had visitors a few years ago, friends of her sire's who came to the castle now and again to breathe in the fresh air and be near the water. Her mother hadn't wanted them to stay, but they'd insisted on spending a single night at the castle. She'd led the young man out to the rocks to show him the wonderful view, and he'd surprised her by grasping her shoulders and spinning her around to face him. He'd planted his cold lips against hers, then proceeded to lick her with his tongue in a most unappealing manner.

She'd pushed him away, but that didn't matter to her mother. As soon as their guests left, her mother had chastised her, saying she'd seen them cavorting out the window. Her mother had refused to hear her side of it, so she'd gone to bed without supper and cried herself to sleep.

About two months later, she'd begun to bleed. The sight of the bright red blood had terrified her. Her mother had seen the blood on her clothing and explained to her that it was the Lord's way of punishing lasses for being free with themselves.

How she prayed God would forgive her soon because she was tired of bleeding every month. She sat on the bed with the pile of rags on her lap, not knowing what to do with them, when the sweetest voice she'd ever heard whispered, "You are bleeding, too?"

CHAPTER EIGHT

R ODDY SWUNG HIS FIST IN a wide arc with a roar, then sat up in his bed.

"What the hell?" Connor sat up in the bed against the opposite wall.

Roddy rubbed his eyes, doing his best to banish the vision of the wild boars chasing him to the edge of the water, forcing him to jump in. The water had looked like it did outside of Rose's keep, wild and deadly, and he'd known he would drown. "Sorry, Connor. 'Twas a nightmare. My apologies. Go back to sleep."

Connor fell back into bed and rolled onto his side, falling asleep almost instantly.

Roddy could not fall back asleep now. Not with images of boar tusks and swirling water dancing in his mind.

The nightmares were getting worse.

They'd assailed him off and on for most of his life, but they'd lingered for long after the battle in which his uncle Alex had nearly lost his life. It had been such a shock to see bodies littering the ground, blood everywhere, and the images had come to him again and again in his dreams. For a while, they'd faded, but they'd come back after Braden's fight with the Lamonts. Why hadn't he gotten used to death? It was part of being a warrior. It was part of *life*.

Now his nightmares always involved water and drowning. He fought to rise to the top, only to wake up gasping for air.

He couldn't stop them, no matter how he tried. He'd tried special potions from his mother, without telling her why she needed them, training his thoughts when he went to bed at night, and talking the problem through, but nothing had helped. Instead, his dreams grew and grew, and of late, they seemed to always involve water. Now, to his delight, this one involved boars *and* drowning. How he wished he'd drowned the beasts.

He had no idea what to do. How could he stop them?

He swung his legs off the side of the bed and set his feet on the floor, resting his elbows on his knees. There was no way he'd fall asleep now.

Forcing himself to his feet, he made his way toward the great hall, creeping down the stairs as quietly as he could, hoping not to awaken anyone. To his surprise, he ran into Braden coming out of the kitchens with a turkey leg in his hand.

His cousin smirked and offered him the treat. "Here. I'll grab another." When they were younger, they'd built a reputation for having insatiable appetites. They'd find a way to eat at one cottage, then go to the next one complaining of starvation. Everyone they ran into muttered on about growing lads and their big appetites, but the words were usually said with an indulgent grin.

"Something's bothering you," Braden said, as he emerged with a second turkey leg. He waved it toward the hearth, indicating they should make their way over to it. "'Tis the only reason you do not sleep, cousin. What is it?"

Roddy ran his free hand down his face as they settled in front of the hearth, its embers still warm. "I had another nightmare."

"About dying?"

"Aye, dying and drowning," he replied, exasperated. Though he had only recently shared his shame with Connor, he'd told Braden a while back, after his friend met Cairstine. He'd needed to tell someone. "I cannot shake this fear of dying. I do not understand it. I could have lost my life to that boar earlier. I was paralyzed with fear. The boar was ready to go for my neck and I froze." He attacked the turkey leg as though it had caused all his problems.

"But you regained your senses and killed the beast, did you not?"

He sighed, unable to explain how helpless—and use-less—he'd felt in that moment. "Aye, but I did it on reflex. It might have gone verra differently. If I don't figure out a solution to my problem, I'll have to request to be taken off the traveling warrior group. I'm afraid I'll not be of any help to anyone. I cannot explain how powerless I become in those moments."

"Do you have something else on your mind that's keeping you from focusing clearly?" The look in Braden's eyes told him his cousin thought he already had the answer.

He took the last bite of the turkey leg and dropped it onto the table in front of him, wiping his mouth with his sleeve. "Aye, you're not wrong. I hardly know Rose, but I cannot get her out of my mind." He tugged on the lock of hair that insisted on falling forward into his eyes.

"Have you seen her again?" They'd arrived at Braden's castle late, after he and his family were abed, and both had been too disturbed by the incident with the boars to seek an audience with their cousin. They'd agreed to do so the next morn.

"Nay, but—"

Braden held up a hand. "Mayhap the story will go down better with some mead." He had finished his own turkey leg, and he took the rubbish to the kitchens and returned with two goblets of mead, handing one to Roddy before he sat down to listen.

"She wasn't there when we returned to the castle," Roddy said. "Her mother informed us she had taken her to Sona Abbey to take her vows." Roddy could tell by the expression on Braden's face that he was as surprised as they had been at this information. "Aye," he continued. "Her mother said she went to the abbey willingly. That she wishes to become a nun. She's in training."

Roddy rubbed his hands together, waiting to see his cousin's reaction.

Braden whistled. "'Tis a tough situation. But if you wish to talk with her, you should seek her out."

"Our next stop was the abbey. They claimed she wasn't there, but I fear they may be holding her there against her will."

"And so you left?" Braden's gaze narrowed on him.

"What else was I to do? We needed to finish our mission of searching the area for other possible places for the Channel."

"Let me explain something to you. I had a bad feeling about Greer Lamont and his wife, or the woman I thought was his wife."

"Cairstine."

"Aye, Cairstine. I didn't like the way he treated her when I first saw them together. And there was something about Cairstine that grabbed me. So I followed them. I waited until Lamont was out of sight before talking to her. She was still guarded, but I understood why. Steenie was with her. The lad had too much fear in his gaze to suit me. Still, she refused my assistance and returned to Muir Castle."

"But you didn't let that stop you." Roddy knew exactly where his cousin was going with this tale. Greer Lamont had controlled Cairstine and their son, Steenie, with an iron fist. She'd been too afraid to leave him—and she hadn't wanted to abandon her castle to the man.

"Nay, I did not. Had I ignored my gut feeling, had I stepped away from her, she would not be my wife now. She would still be a prisoner in her own castle."

"So what should I do?" Roddy asked, getting out of his chair to start pacing, his fingers still playing with the lock of hair that would not stay put.

"Find a way to sneak in and search the premises," Braden said. "Daniel sent word that he'll arrive on the morrow.

We'll bring him with us. There will be four of us. We can find out if she's there, and if she's not, we'll find out where she is. We have to uncover anything we can about the Channel of Dubh. We won't have much time, but we can do what we can for Rose."

"And if I find her? What do I do? Kidnap her? What if she doesn't wish to come with me? There is a wee communication issue between us." Was he daft to be this entranced by a lass who couldn't speak with him?

"Nay, you'll not kidnap her until we have a slew of warriors there to protect us. First you must find out if she's being kept there against her will. Then we must find out why. We also need to find out how many guards they keep at the abbey. 'Tis an abbey, so we must be verra careful. But this abbey and the abbey south are the only two possibilities we have at this point. One or both of them could be part of the Channel. Once we have all the information we need, we'll return to Clan Grant and make a plan. You'll get no support from Uncle Alex without answers."

Roddy thought about everything his cousin had said, then nodded his agreement. "Aye, you speak wisely, Braden. We'll await Daniel's arrival, then go back."

"You feel better already, do you not? Now that the decision has been made."

He smiled. "Aye, I do feel much better."

"Then follow your hunches about Rose MacDole."

———◆———

Rose stared into her friend's eyes. How she wished she could ask her friend what she meant. Did she know that God made her bleed every month? Did she know what kind of sin she'd committed to make it so?

"I have my courses, too. 'Tis why I'm here," Constance said, pulling Rose down to sit on the bed next to her. "I get terrible cramps every month. I moan in my sleep." She continued to hold Rose's hand. "Do you have cramps, too?"

Rose shook her head no, squeezing Constance's hand to let her know she felt badly about her cramps.

"I hate it, but all lasses go through it. There's naught we can do to stop it, though they do cause me terrible pain," she said, holding her belly to show her where the pain was the worst. "Right here is the pain. Constant." Then she looked at Rose. "I hate the bleeding worst of all. 'Tis disgusting, is it not?"

Rose was so excited she didn't know what to ask first. She'd believed her mother without question, thinking all along that the bleeding was her punishment for being weak and bad.

Taking her time, Rose traced the word "mother" on the bed. Then she imitated kissing, hoping her friend would comprehend her meaning. Lastly, she pointed to her feminine parts.

Constance frowned, rubbing her forehead. "I'm sorry, Rose, but what would kissing have to do with your courses? You're not married, so I don't think you did what married couples do."

Rose mouthed the word "bad." Then she pursed her lips in a kiss again.

Constance grinned and whispered, "I don't think kissing is bad. With the right lad, 'tis quite nice. I kissed one boy I really liked. His lips were warm and sweet and he held me in his arms as though he'd never let me go." Her eyes lit up with the memory. "He was so nice, but he returned to England."

Rose mouthed, "God?"

Her friend shook her head. "God wouldn't think kissing is bad. God wants couples to marry and have children. Kissing is part of love. It's how you know if you and the lad you fancy suit. Who told you that?"

She mouthed the word "mother."

"Oh, Rose. Are you saying that your mother told you

that God thinks you're bad for kissing a boy?"

Nodding frantically, Rose pointed again to her female parts.

"Your mother told you kissing a boy would make you bleed?" Constance's jaw stayed open after that last comment.

Rose wanted so badly to explain the entire situation to her friend. Who else could she talk to about it? This entire fabricated tale had come from someone who should have loved her. Someone she should have been able to trust.

Rose picked up a book beside the bed, and her hands flew from word to word, from picture to picture, as she tried to explain everything to her friend.

After watching Rose for a few minutes, Constance finally stopped her by grasping her shoulder. "Rose, are you saying your mother told you that you bleed every month because you were caught kissing a boy? That kissing is bad, and God is punishing you by making you bleed?"

Rose closed her eyes and fell onto the bed with exhaustion. She nodded briefly, sighing with relief that her friend had understood her. Then, wanting to express one final thought, she sat up and pointed to the picture of the abbey on the wall.

"And she sent you here because she thinks you were bad?" Constance said with a gasp. "Not because you wish to be a nun?"

Rose nodded, tears running down her face.

Constance pulled her up to stand. She embraced her, then pulled back so she could explain everything to Rose without being overheard. She whispered, "Nay, those are lies. Mayhap you misunderstood what she was telling you, but 'tis not true at all." She pointed back and forth to the pictures and words, shaking her head vehemently. "We only bleed because Eve...never mind. I'll explain that to you later." She paused for a moment while she gripped Rose's hands. "Do you know how babies are made?"

Rose shook her head.

"We have much to discuss, my friend. But that can wait until another day. I'm tired." She pointed to her bed. "Sleep now?" she put her hands together next to her head and closed her eyes. "We'll talk more on the morrow?"

Rose nodded. She needed time to process all she'd just learned. She gave Constance a squeeze, made the sign they'd agreed upon to mean "thank you," then moved to her own bed.

Twenty minutes later, she was still awake. She listened to Constance's soft, rhythmic breathing, telling her that her friend was sound asleep. Rose stared at the ceiling, an unusual feeling coursing through her, very different than anything she'd ever experienced before.

Instead of fear, she felt strength.

Instead of doubt, she felt confidence.

Instead of feeling anxious, she felt calm.

Her mother had lied to her. She'd created a cruel story to justify mistreating her and sending her off to the abbey.

And she'd done it all with a smile and a gleam in her eyes.

When she was certain Constance was sound asleep, Rose climbed out of bed and moved over to the small window, staring up at the nearly full moon and the surrounding stars. In that moment, she made a vow to herself.

She would never be weak again, nor would she bend to her mother's will.

Rose MacDole had just been reborn as a woman of strength and conviction.

A woman who had a plan.

It was about time she used her disability to her advantage. Though she was still confused by her mother's motivations for treating her so cruelly, she clearly had a reason for wanting to get Rose out of the castle. She'd find out. She'd become a spy to all that took place whenever her mother was around. Perhaps she'd sneak out one night, borrow a horse, and spy on her mother, or go to the caves and see if there were any more boats. Something odd was taking place near MacDole Castle, and she hated to admit it, but she suspected her mother knew all about it. Out of the corner of her eye, she caught sight of someone sneaking around in the gardens below the window.

About to start her new mission, she made the decision to begin by sneaking out of the infirmary.

Who was slinking about in the gardens?

CHAPTER NINE

RODDY TOOK A DEEP BREATH, staring up at the moon, wondering if there was too much moonlight for their venture. Daniel had arrived yesterday. They had informed him of the situation, they'd all searched the area the next morning, and now they were returning to the abbey. Daniel had insisted they wait until nightfall.

Connor and Braden had agreed to patrol the periphery of the abbey. Daniel would join him inside the abbey. Roddy only hoped his nickname, Ghost, would prove accurate.

"Ghost, you lead the way," he said, "I've not done much spy work." He couldn't stop one side of his mouth from curling up. Perhaps instead of being a warrior he could work for the Scottish Crown like Maggie and Will did. They weren't true spies. Their purpose was to carry out instructions made by King Alexander, who was dealing with so many family matters that he wasn't often heard from of late. At least as a spy, he wouldn't need to face death regularly.

Daniel said, "You must be like a deer—graceful yet quick."

"Uncle Logan is graceful and quick?" he asked with a snort. The last thing word he would use to describe the man was graceful. He was more like a bull, stomping and grunting his way through everything.

"Nay, not like Uncle Logan. Have you ever watched Aunt Gwyneth? She runs like a deer and is as graceful as any dancer. Uncle Logan wouldn't be much of a spy without her. You must travel without being seen or heard. 'Tis the trick."

"I'll do my best. Where do we start?" They stood outside a fence near the rear of the abbey. The curtain wall didn't extend all the way around the abbey. The only barrier was a tall fence, which would make their task that much easier.

"This is easy to climb," Daniel said. "Better than a curtain wall, though that hedge may be a bastard to get through. I'd say the lasses probably sleep on the second floor and the monks in one of the separate buildings. What's in the building outside the fence? Do you know?"

"That building houses guests. You don't want to go inside. Trust me."

"Then we ignore it. We'd do best to start at opposite ends and move toward the middle. So the lass won't be able to talk to us, eh? It must be a struggle for her to communicate. 'Tis unfortunate or she could spy for us on the inside of the abbey."

Roddy glanced down at Daniel's arm, the one he'd lost below the elbow to a sword injury at a young age. "You've learned to get along with your issues. Can she not do the same?"

"Well said, my friend. I'll start at the front because 'twill be a wee bit difficult getting past the guards. You go to the garden in the back and see if you can find a window to climb into. Meet me back at this location in one half hour."

Roddy nodded. "Godspeed."

He watched as Daniel sprinted away without making a sound or moving a blade of grass. Graceful as a deer, indeed. When Daniel slipped out of sight, Roddy proceeded through the garden to one of the trees, hoping he could climb it to gain access to the second floor. The garden, full of flowering vines, fragrant fruit trees, and well-placed benches, would be quite beautiful during the day.

He'd just made it to the tree when he heard a door open not far away, one well hidden behind the hedge bushes. He froze, hiding as best he could, but his future as a spy was clearly ill-fated—he'd barely managed to conceal himself when a young lass emerged from the door, closing it silently behind her.

Rose.

He would know her profile anywhere. Not wishing to frighten her, he waited until she was nearly by him before stepping out in front of her.

He startled her, but her face broke into a wide grin instantly, something that pleased him immensely. He couldn't stop a smile from rising on his own face. He held his hand out to her, hoping she would take it, but instead she launched herself at him and wrapped her arms around him in a most unladylike bear hug.

When he broke away, he whispered, "Are you hale?"

She nodded, rubbing her hands up and down his arms, showing him how glad she was to see him.

He took her by the hand and led her away from the abbey to a bench at the edge of the large garden. Though it was dark, the moon was bright enough to guide them. Once he sat down and she nestled in close, he whispered, "I have so many things I wish to ask you. Someday, I'll teach you how to read and write. Most of my cousins know because my aunt Maddie insisted on teaching all of us."

Out of nowhere, a tousled head popped up from the plants near the doorway Rose had used to leave the abbey. Rose wasn't bothered at all, instead waving the lass closer to them. He lifted her gaze with a finger under her chin. "Do you know her?"

"Aye," the girl said as she came closer. "I'm her friend, Constance." She set her hand on Rose's arm until she had her attention, then asked, "Does he know the truth?"

Rose nodded, her eyes misting.

"Know the truth about what? I came because I wish to know if she's here against her will."

"Hush, and I'll tell you what she's told me. First, you

know she can hear, correct?"

"Aye, she told me that already. But I have many questions I'd like answered."

Rose patted his hand, tugged on his earlobe, and pointed to Constance. *Listen.* "Go ahead," he said.

Constance began, "Rose joined us about a sennight ago. I've been teaching her how to read, and we've also made up some of our own signs for words. I've also been able to use picture books to help Rose get her words across."

He squeezed Rose's shoulder and said, "Good."

"We just had quite a conversation, if you will. Rose's mother saw her kissing a lad some time ago, and she made her think that it was bad. She said God would punish her, and then…" She paused. "Are you the lad?"

Rose held both of her hands up, palms facing out, shaking them to indicate he was not the lad. He couldn't help but wonder who it had been. A sudden feeling of jealousy surged through him. But he forced himself to pay attention to the matters at hand since he didn't have much time.

"Well, anyway, she made Rose think that…" she paused, blushing as she looked at Rose, who indicated with an urgent wave of her hand that she should continue.

Constance took a deep breath, then reached for Rose's hand before she finished speaking. "Her mother told her God would make her bleed every month until he forgave her for her transgression."

Roddy was quiet for a moment, unable to process what Constance had just told him. She couldn't be referring to a woman's monthly courses, could she? Why, that would be…that was…what kind of monster would tell a young lass such a thing? Nay. He had to be wrong.

"You mean she convinced her that the reason she bleeds every month as a woman is because the Lord is angry with her?"

"Aye, apparently she caught her kissing another lad a few days back. She sent her here because she had sinned, not because she wants to be a nun. She told her that if she stops bleeding every month, it will mean the Lord has forgiven her and she can return home."

Roddy frowned. "The second lad is me. Rose, I'm so sorry..."

Rose shook her head with a vehemence that told him her time away from home had been good for her. She'd gained some confidence. Then the larger meaning behind Constance's words struck him hard. "But that would mean she would be here..."

Constance filled in his thoughts. "Aye, that would mean she'd never go home."

Roddy brought his gaze up to meet Rose's, trying so hard to hide the revulsion he felt for her mother. What kind of twisted creature would tell their child such a bold lie? "I'm so sorry, Rose. I'm stunned. Why would your mother want you out of the castle?"

Rose made a series of gestures and made a few words with her lips, but he couldn't understand what she was trying to say. "Constance? Are you comprehending any of her signs? Reading her lips?"

Constance shook her head, but then two of the words Rose was trying to get across finally registered.

"Boat" and "night."

A strange sensation crawled down his spine. Rose herself thought there was a connection between her mother and the boat she'd seen at the dock.

As soon as Rose's tears started, he said, "Enough, Constance. I don't want to frustrate her any longer. Those two words tell me much. Why don't you go back inside?"

The girl shot him a look, then shifted her attention to Rose. "Do you want to stay with him?"

Rose held up her ten fingers.

"All right. Ten minutes. I'll go inside and wait, but I'll be just inside the door."

As soon as Constance took her leave, Rose fell against

Roddy and sobbed. Hell, he didn't know what to do, so he just held her while she cried. Her head rested underneath his chin and he took in her sweet floral scent, breathing it in deeper. It reminded him of the violet hue of her eyes. He brushed the hair back from her face, rubbing his thumb across her cheek.

A few minutes later, she stopped crying and pushed away from his chest, her eyes red and her cheeks drenched. Somehow, she was still the most gorgeous woman he'd ever seen. She peered up at him and touched her lips with her fingers and then moved them to his lips.

Confused, he said, "Kiss?"

She nodded, her gaze forlorn and confused.

"Do you want me to kiss you?" He pointed at himself, then to her.

She nodded, the confused expression changing to one of hope.

"You understand that the Lord won't think badly of us for kissing?"

A brief smile crossed her lips and she nodded.

Roddy cupped her face and covered her lips with his, tasting her slowly so as not to frighten her. He moved his lips over hers and she parted her lips just enough for him to slip his tongue inside, giving him the chance to taste her. He could tell she was an innocent, so he did his best to move slowly rather than ravaging her the way he wished to do.

Rose melded her body against his, and he wrapped his arms around her back to tug her closer. At first, she was stiff, but once her body met his, it was as if a match had been lit within her. Her passion ignited his own.

He couldn't get enough of his sweet Rose, but he knew he had to stop. He did not wish to cause any more trouble for her, especially since they were inside the walls of the abbey, so he ended the kiss. She whimpered, a slight gasp in the back of her throat that fueled his desire.

He forced himself to set her away from him and then pointed to the door. "You must go back. Constance is waiting for you." He couldn't help but wonder what other twisted views the lass had been taught about relationships between men and women, but he wouldn't upset her any more this night.

She took his hand in hers and led him over to the door that led into the abbey. Leaning against him as they strolled, she sighed, which he took as a good sign. When they arrived, she stood on her tiptoes and kissed him briefly on the lips, then waved goodbye to him.

He asked, "How old?" Pointed to her chest.

Constance opened the door and said, "She's ten and seven, nearly ten and eight." She blushed a bit, having revealed she was listening to them, and closed the door again.

He pointed to his chest and said, "I'll be back."

She smiled and opened the door, looking back at him over her shoulder as she slipped inside. That last fleeting glimpse of the beautiful lass tempted him to grab her and never let go. He wished to help her, to fix this chaos that had thrown her life into disarray. He couldn't imagine what she might be thinking.

What could be worse than your own mother lying to you to get rid of you?

———◆———

Roddy and Daniel met up with Connor and Braden in front of the abbey, but Braden motioned for them to move a distance away before talking. They followed the path until they reached a clearing near a bubbling burn, where they stopped to water their horses and share their discoveries.

"What did you learn?" Braden asked.

"I found Rose," Roddy replied, "and discovered she's there because her mother forced her. The MacDole woman told her she's sinned and has to beg the Lord for forgiveness."

Daniel's jaw dropped open. "That sweet thing I saw running into the infirmary has sinned? I don't believe it."

Roddy jolted with surprise. "You made it all the way to the infirmary?"

"Aye, and I saw the two of them sneak back in. One lass with really dark hair and one with curly red hair. And one looking as though she'd been thoroughly kissed, if I had to guess." Daniel winked at the other two lads, but Roddy did not respond.

"And what else did you discover?" he pressed.

"Och, that there are at most thirty guards, quite a large number for an abbey this size. This makes me question the activities going on here. The priest and abbess who run the abbey have one verra large benefactor who controls much of what they do, but I could not uncover that person's name."

"Could be anyone," Connor noted.

"I will find out when we go back," Daniel said, an impish grin dancing across his face.

"We will be going back?" Braden asked.

"We sure will. Roddy will insist on it." He shot him a meaningful look. "And even if he didn't, there's most certainly something going on there. I could feel it in every person I saw. They're all afraid of something."

"Aye," Connor said. "Something to do with Abbey of the Angels, no doubt. Who are the other neighbors in the area, Braden? Do you know them?"

"Some, but not all. There's one family north of me, but I would not call them wealthy. No one directly to the west because the landscape is so poor. Loki is east of us, but a bit of a stretch. Don't know who's to the south."

"Why haven't you sent out any patrols yet?" Daniel asked.

The other three chuckled. "Braden does not have many guards to patrol for him yet. He's gained mayhap five. Loki patrols for him on occasion."

Daniel stroked his chin as he thought. "Hmmm. Mayhap I should stay with you for a while. 'Twould be interesting."

"You are most welcome to join me. I have plenty of empty chambers in the castle and even two huts remain unclaimed," Braden offered. "Think on it."

"Back to our topic, Rose mentioned something else interesting," Roddy said.

"How so?" Connor interrupted wryly. "Has she suddenly learned to speak?"

"Nay. We had an interpreter in a sense. She's been working with another lass from the abbey. They've developed their own systems of signs and they also use picture books to communicate with each other. Constance was able to tell me most of the story, and it's not a good one." That caught their attention, and he had to force himself to calm down as a righteous fury blossomed inside him. Steeling himself, he told them what he knew.

"So her own mother sent her to the abbey for the rest of her life without her agreement?" Connor asked. "I thought Lady MacDole was a nasty woman, but I didn't suspect anything like this."

"Aye," Roddy said, "And she's only ten and seven."

Dead silence met his revelation. He didn't blame his cousins. It was just as shocking to him to speak this truth as it was for them to hear it.

Braden shook his head, staring at the ground, and whispered, "Unbelievable."

"Anything else?" Connor whispered.

"Aye. I asked her if she knew of any reason why her mother wouldn't want her at the castle, and she became quite animated over something. Neither Constance nor I could make much of what she was saying, but I did pick up two words. Boat and night. It's clear she suspects her mother's involved with whatever's happening beneath MacDole Castle."

Braden said, "There must be something going on at the castle, some reason her mother wanted her out. This could all be connected. We must follow up on this."

"Aye, my feelings exactly," Connor agreed. "In fact, I think we ought to head back to Muir Castle and send a messenger to Will and Maggie. They need to be here soon."

Three other heads nodded in agreement.

They took off at a good canter. With luck, they'd arrive back at Braden's shortly after midnight. Unfortunately, luck wasn't with them that night.

They hadn't gone far when they were attacked.

Eight reivers to the four of them.

CHAPTER TEN

RODDY NEARLY CHOKED WITH FEAR. One rider headed straight for him, his weapon raised.

Connor cut the reiver down with one swing of his sword. "Roddy, wake up!" he shouted.

It felt as if everything around Roddy had sped up—but he'd slowed down. As if the very air around him had grown heavier. He stared at the melee, swinging his sword, but not with a fraction of the drive and conviction he had in the lists.

He managed to knock one reiver off his horse while Braden took down two each. Daniel stuck his sword in the belly of another of their attackers. That only left only one.

And he was charging straight toward Roddy.

The reiver had already ascertained which of them was the weakest link—and it wasn't the warrior with only one arm.

The reiver swung his sword from the side aiming to cut Roddy in half, but he blocked the swing and plunged his sword deep into the man's chest, killing him instantly.

That was the last one.

The other three bellowed and shouted as they glanced at the eight men they'd taken down, but Roddy couldn't celebrate.

Anyone looking at him would guess he panted from exertion, but he didn't. He couldn't catch his breath because the fear of nearly dying had once again overpowered him, and he fought to gain his equilibrium back.

When would this stop?

———•———

Rose woke up the next morning with a new sense of purpose.

Roddy's kiss had awakened something inside her—something she wished to explore further. This was someone who was not only kind to her, but someone who believed in her.

Someone who hadn't been stopped by her mother.

She would stay strong for herself, but also for Roddy. They deserved the chance to explore their relationship further. If she could just find a way out of the abbey, they could have that chance.

She would join Clan Grant if they would accept her. Anything to get away from her mother.

She also needed to focus on learning how to better communicate. Constance had helped her immensely, but she'd still struggled to get her words across to Roddy.

Frustration exhausted her.

When she climbed out of bed, she did so carefully so as not to awaken Constance, who was still sleeping soundly. She made her way to the nun's area, to the private chamber where she could finish her morning ablutions.

She had three goals: to finish learning to read, to find out for certain why her mother wished to get rid of her, and to get to know Roddy Grant better. She'd done her best to explain to Roddy that she'd remembered something about the boat's visits to the dock. It had occurred to her that her mother always told her to go inside on the nights the boat came. It had never stopped her from sneaking out, however. While she'd never seen much, she'd heard a strange noise coming from the area around the docks one night.

Lassies crying. She hadn't been able to identify the sound then, but now she was certain she was right. What had the men done with the lasses? Where were they sending them?

And what did her mother have to do with all of it?

She had a feeling Roddy and his cousins were the only ones who could help her answer her questions.

When she finished her ablutions, Sister Murreall came along and said, "I know you cannot hear me, lass, but brush your hair and put on the nicer gown. Your mother is here, and I'm sure she'll be up to see you before she leaves." She took her hand and said, "Come along with me. I'll find you something to wear."

Rose was careful not to react, though she wished to run out of the infirmary. Nay, she wished to run out of the abbey and keep running until she was far, far away.

Sister Murreall led her down the passageway, selected a nice gown for her from the ones hanging in her chamber, then brought her back to the sick room. "Here, this should do nicely. Your mother is with the abbess presently, so no need to hurry. Our regular gowns aren't nice enough for you to wear to meet your mother. This one you brought with you will show off your eyes." The kind nun meandered back down the passageway, muttering to herself. "I do not know why I insist on talking to someone who cannot hear me. I must be daft in my old age."

Rose wished to hug the nun, but the woman left as quickly and quietly as she'd come. Constance sat up, rubbing the sleep from her eyes.

"What is it? Why did Sister Murreall bring you back to our chamber for a nicer gown?"

Rose gave her the sign for her mother, tracing an M in the palm of her hand, then pointed to the ground.

Constance groaned. "Your mother is here." She fell back onto her bed as Rose removed her night rail and reached for a shift and the wool gown. "What will we do?"

Rose hated to lie to Constance, but she feared her friend would insist on coming if she were to admit she intended to eavesdrop.

To protect both of them, she merely told Constance she was going for a walk.

She crept down the back staircase, listening for anyone along the way, but since it was time for mass, she didn't expect to see people moving about. Once she made it to the passageway without being seen, she hurried to the end, toward the chambers reserved for Father Seward and Mother Abbess.

No one was around, so she crept stealthily until she was outside the mother abbess's door. The room was silent, so she continued on to the priest's chamber. There, she heard voices, so she settled in a small alcove and listened.

Father Seward said, "She is doing quite fine, but I believe you are too hard on her, my lady."

Her mother said, "I'm quite worried about her. She takes it verra hard when she is unable to communicate with others. 'Tis why I recommended she be left in her own private chamber, and that all her meals should be brought to her."

"I believe you expect too much from her," Mother Marion said. "She's not much more than a child because of her failings. I assigned another student to help her find her way here. 'Tis important she feel welcome. She's lived a sheltered, lonely life. Would you not agree?"

"But that is my fear. Once she is among others, they'll mock her because she cannot hear, so 'twould be best if she were left alone. Or assign her to work in the kitchens, and she can chop vegetables all day. Being around other lasses, lasses who can do what she cannot, it is just too painful. Have the other lasses taunted her yet?"

There was a pause, after which Mother Marion quietly admitted, "Aye, there was an incident. But I fear 'tis only because of her inability to communicate and her lack of experience with other young people."

"And since it has already happened, you can see that I am right," her mother insisted loftily. "I want her kept away from the others."

Father Seward cleared his throat. "I would suggest we

teach her to read. She could point to words to get her message across. Mayhap someday she could learn to write. That would give her the means to communicate, the chance to have a more meaningful life. She could at least read books."

"Absolutely not," her mother replied. "You would upset her by giving her something that is too difficult for her to learn."

Someone gasped, then Mother Abbess said, "Are you suggesting your daughter doesn't have the mental ability to learn to read?"

"I know my daughter," Rose's mother insisted. "She is a lovely child, but she is... How shall I say this without appearing cruel." The silence echoed loudly, and Rose had to use all her self-control to keep herself from pushing the door open and screaming at her mother.

If she only could scream.

"Stupid. I feel horrible saying the word, but she is not an intelligent child. I fear reading would be too difficult for her, and I'll not have it. I'll visit her today, if you please."

Rose knew she should leave to avoid being caught, but the chairs had not yet moved. She hesitated, not wanting to miss anything her mother said.

"She's in the infirmary at present," Father Seward explained.

"Why is she in the infirmary?"

"Because a cruel bunch of girls embarrassed her over her courses in the great hall. I took the liberty of escorting her to the infirmary. I have taken care of the worst of the offenders. 'Twill not happen again."

A chair clattered against the floor. "You're to leave her in her own chamber as I instructed. Do not coddle my child. I'll not have it! If you do not do as I say, I'll cut my payment in half."

Her mother must have stood up, so Rose readied herself to race back down the passageway. The last thing she wished to do was be caught in such a position.

"Verra well," Mother Marion said. "We'll take care of the situation."

"Now, I'd like to see my child." Her voice was once again as sweet as could be. "I'm sure she needs a mother's comforting after this debacle. Lead the way, please."

Someone cleared a throat. "About that payment, my lady," Father Seward said.

Rose didn't need to hear anything about the coin her mother was bribing them to keep her here against her will, so she hurried down the passageway and back up to the infirmary.

A fury blossomed deep in her belly, begging to be let loose. If she could shout, she'd save all of her shouting for her mother. She was *not* stupid.

Who else could manage to keep her mother's secrets? Anyone with a weaker mind would have succumbed long ago.

How many other lasses would be capable of convincing the entire world that they were deaf when they weren't? Anyone else would have made a mistake, turned an ear to a loud noise, reacted to something someone said, or done something that would lead others to believe that she could indeed hear.

She'd done it quite easily and had never been questioned. How could the evil woman not see that took intelligence? She slipped inside the door to the chamber in the infirmary, nodded to Constance and took a seat on the edge of her bed. Soon, she could hear the voices of the abbess and her mother, who had apparently been joined by Sister Murreall. They drew close but Rose said nothing to Constance, not wanting her to suspect where she'd been.

"They're coming!" Constance pointed and let her know three people were approaching the room.

A light knock landed on the door, but Rose ignored it.

The abbess called out a greeting that only Constance responded to. Standing and folding her hands in front of her, Constance said, "Come in, Mother Abbess. 'Tis most lovely to see you this morn."

Rose acted startled when they entered, another one of her well-practiced coverups.

"Oh my dearest," her mother cried, hurrying to her side, sitting on the bed, and wrapping her arms around her. "I've heard you've had a difficult time of late. I'm so sorry the other girls have been unpleasant to you." Once she embraced her daughter, her arms clutching too tightly for comfort, she addressed Constance. "If you do not mind, I'd like some time alone with my daughter. I'm sure she'd appreciate it if you left us for a short time." She gave her best practiced smile to the abbess and to Constance.

Nothing could be further from the truth.

Mother Abbess said, "How do you fare this morn, Rose?" Then she fussed, realizing she had spoken to a deaf person as though she would answer. To make up for it, she said to Constance, "Does she seem better this morn?"

Constance quickly answered her question before she headed out the door. "She does seem to feel a wee bit more herself. I think I can return to my regular chamber today, Mother Abbess. May I come back for my things later?"

"Why of course, my dear. Do as you are comfortable doing." The abbess gave her shoulder a pat. Before following her out of the room, she asked, "Will you be needing anything else, Lady MacDole?"

"Nay, I am fine. I just wish to spend time with my dear daughter. I do miss her so." She smiled as she wrapped her arm around Rose's shoulders, leaning in as if to give her a hug.

"Verra well. I will take my leave. If you need anything at all, send for the sister. She'll assist you." The abbess bowed briefly and left, shutting the door with a resounding click.

Rose watched as her mother stood and made her way to the door, ensuring it was indeed shut. She never took her eyes off the woman because she now knew her for what she was—a liar.

Even so, Rose was completely surprised by her mother's next action.

Lady MacDole spun on her heel, swinging her arm in a wide arc, and struck her so hard across her cheek that she fell back onto the bed.

Her mother had never struck her before. Her hand flew up to protect the now stinging skin on her face, afraid she was about to be a hit a second time.

What could she do to protect herself? She was stuck in a building where the abbess, the nuns, and the priest were all under her mother's control. All receiving her coin, apparently. She pushed up on her elbows and used her feet to maneuver her back up against the wall, anything to put space between her and the cruel woman.

Her mother's voice changed into the vilest of whispers, her tone grating and the fury in her eyes unlike anything Rose had ever seen or heard. "Look what you've done! I sent you here to beg for forgiveness from our dear Lord because of your whoring sins. Apparently, you haven't done what He expected of you because here you are bleeding again. I hear it has been a most difficult time for you, so you must have angered our Lord even more. You will not learn how to read. You are here to beg for absolution of your sins, not to make friends with anyone. You will not coddle yourself, and you will not spend your time with other young people. Do you understand me?"

Rose nodded, still protecting her face.

Her mother leaned over and grasped her underarm, squeezing it hard enough to make Rose wish she could cry out. She whispered in Rose's ear, "Do you? Because I haven't forgotten my promise to you. If you don't behave as you should, I'll send you out to an island where no one will ever find you. I'll leave you to die a slow death of starvation...or mayhap you'll be attacked by a wild animal.

Do not think I won't do it. I've had enough of you inter-fering in my life. I didn't want you when you were born, and I don't want you now. Do as I say or you will regret it."

Rose nodded her agreement. What else could she do?

Her mother stood, her eyes still boring into Rose. She shook herself as if to regain her composure and readied herself to leave. "Now, I will take my leave. When I return next, I expect to find you in a chamber alone, praying for forgiveness. I have given the father and abbess strict instructions that you are to see no one, and you are to receive all your meals in your chamber. You will be sent to do hard labor for four hours a day, even when you bleed."

Her mother turned to go out the door, but then turned back around. "I see the shock on your face, child, and I understand it." Her voice had returned to a normal tone in case anyone overheard their discussion. "You were coddled by your father, but he's no longer here to protect you. I am all you have. Please do not make the mistake of underes-timating me."

The last sentence came out in a whisper. Then she turned and stalked out of the room.

The old Rose would have sobbed.

The new Rose swore she'd get her revenge, even against her own mother.

CHAPTER ELEVEN

———◆———

RODDY WOKE UP IN A cold sweat, swinging his arms. Connor yelled at him. "Roddy, what the hell? You're yelling like a wolf caught in nettles."

He did his best to slow his breathing. Fighting to get to the surface of a body of water was no different than fighting a giant beast. In fact, his shoulders nearly ached from swimming to the surface over and over again, never to arrive. "Sorry, another nightmare. I'm fine. Didn't mean to wake you." He climbed off the bed and stalked out of the chamber he shared with Connor at Braden's house.

Connor grunted as he rolled over, or so Roddy would guess. He'd already shut the door behind him and made haste for the stairs. The pace he'd set was punishing, and he forced himself to slow his steps until his breathing slowed also. Wiping the sweat from his forehead, he took a deep, slow breath as the memories of his nightmare returned to him.

Water again. He had been submerged underwater, unable to get to the surface in time.

He found something to drink and fell into a chair in front of the hearth. A few moments later, he was surprised to hear footsteps coming toward him from the tower, where his aunt and uncle now lived.

Uncle Brodie stopped as soon as he noticed Roddy by the hearth. "You are hale, nephew?"

Roddy nodded, leaning forward to rest his elbows on his knees. "Aye, just a nightmare. Woke me enough that I hopped out of bed." He took a swig of the ale he'd poured himself.

His heartbeat had nearly returned to normal. The water had felt so real, his ears rang with the dullness being deep in a loch would give you. He knew those sensations well. He'd grown up on a loch.

Uncle Brodie pulled up a chair and said, "What's troubling you? Anything specific?"

Roddy let out his breath. He'd known his uncle would prod him for more information. The people in his family looked after one another.

"I've been having nightmares occasionally about drowning. I'm in water and can't reach the top."

"Why do you suppose you've had the dreams of late?" Uncle Brodie asked, finding his own goblet of ale to swill.

"Not sure, though mayhap 'tis related to something else I've been experiencing." He paused, doing his best to think over his words before he went any further. Though he'd told his cousins and Rose about his problem, he had not yet shared it with anyone from the older generation. Telling Uncle Brodie would make it feel more real.

"Would you like to share your troubles with me? These old bones have seen more than you have. I'd like to think I've gained some wisdom from it." He gave Roddy a lopsided grin.

The last thing he'd ever think was that any of his uncles were too old to be of use. His father and his uncles had taught him so much. Perhaps Uncle Brodie might have an idea of how to help him, how to end his problem. "The last few times I've come under attack, I've panicked and frozen." He glanced at his uncle to see if he looked shocked, but it was impossible to read his expression. "It happened when we were attacked by boars and then again when we were attacked by reivers." He rubbed his hands together, a gesture he did whenever he didn't know what to make of a situation. He waited to see how his uncle would respond.

Uncle Brodie asked, "Did I not hear that you took one

of the reivers out?"

"Aye, but only when he was nearly upon me. I should have been more aggressive. Any man trained in the Grant lists would have been, but I froze and didn't move until he was nearly upon me. Connor yelled at me to wake up."

"And is that why you finally protected yourself?"

This thought puzzled him. Was that why he'd finally swung his weapon? Because Connor had yelled at him, pulling him out of his panic? "Nay, I think 'twas sheer instinct. Swing or die."

"Then I'd not worry on it. Your instincts are still strong. You'll not allow someone to best you. You've been well-trained and have practiced hard in the lists. That never leaves you. Now, tell me about the nightmares."

Roddy considered his uncle's words. Could he be correct? With a deep sigh, he admitted, "I fall into water and can't find my way back to the surface. I struggle to rise, but I cannot make it."

"Is it similar to the time your sire had to pull you out of the loch?"

Roddy stared at his uncle, trying to recall the incident he referred to, but he could not. "I don't recall…"

"In your loch, the one you swam in all summer. I recall your sire saying he had to go in after a couple of you. You don't remember?"

Roddy tried, but he had no memory of being saved from drowning by his sire. "Nay, I don't recall."

"Mayhap you should ask him about it when you return to Clan Grant. I cannot recall the details because I was not there. But I'm sure your sire remembers. I'd remember if 'twas one of my own."

Roddy rubbed his hand across the scruff of his beard.

Seems as though he would be heading back to Clan Grant soon. He needed answers to his questions.

———◆———

Rose tiptoed down the moonlit path later that night. Sister Murreall had taken away all of the books that morning—and Constance had been forced to leave for another chamber.

Sister Murreall had shaken her head and told them. "There'll be no more of these books for either of you. You must focus on training to become a servant of the Lord." Only she'd muttered something quite different to herself as she made her way down the hall. "I dinnae see what the trouble could be about a lass learning to read, especially one who cannot hear or speak."

Before Constance was forced to leave the room, they were given a minute alone together. "I don't understand why they don't want me to continue to help you with your lessons," Constance said bitterly. "If we can read, then we can learn more about the Bible."

Rose made the sign for her mother.

"Your mother? She's not verra nice, is she? Is that why we're being separated?"

Rose nodded, refusing to cry over the situation. Instead, she would focus all her energy on getting out of the abbey. She wasn't sure where she'd go, but she had to find Roddy. He would help her find a place to stay. Perhaps Clan Grant would accept her for who she was and not try to change her or punish her. No matter what, Constance would always be a part of her. The lass had such a sweet, generous soul.

"Is that also why you must sleep alone and stay in your room?"

Rose nodded, but then indicated that she would not follow the rules set out for her. She would find her way out, even if it were at night. She gave Constance a swift hug.

"Euphemie won't be pleased that she won't have you around to taunt any more. That's the only good that will come of this. You take care, Rose. Best friends we'll be forever. I promise."

Much as she tried, she couldn't stop the misting in her eyes as she watched her dear friend retreat down the passageway, her possessions in her arm.

She'd spent the next hours alone, pondering all that had transpired, and the only thing she could continue to feel was the need to get away.

Far away. At home, her mother had controlled her, but she'd always been able to escape outside. Being cooped up inside was more than she could handle. Once she crept down the staircase and out the door, she stopped for a moment to breathe in the fresh night air. It was a lovely Scottish night, and the sounds of the outdoors were music to her ears. She continued to walk slowly and softly down the garden path, contemplating what she should do next and where she should go.

An owl hooted so loudly she jumped. Swiveling her head to take in the area around her, she was pleased to see no one had been there to notice her reaction to the loud sound.

When she reached the end of the path, the owl sat on the branch above her. It had golden eyes, and its feathers were glorious shades of brown and black and gray. Why didn't humans have such a mixture of colors in their hair?

As if to speak to her, its beak opened and a slight "hoo" came out. How Rose wished she could communicate with the regal bird. She watched its movement—how it stood so tall, how its head moved without moving his body. It rotated its head to look at a nearby bird but then swiveled back to stare at her.

Under its golden gaze, she felt as if her father were with her, as if he'd found a way to communicate with her from beyond.

The owl's talons reached out as if it wished to sit on her arm, but she'd heard how powerful bird's talons could be. She reached into the inside of her gown for the linen square she'd tucked in there. Shaking it out, she then settled it on her forearm and moved closer to the owl to see if he would actually perch on her arm.

The bird stared at her, then away, then stared at her again. Finally, it reached out one talon, touching her arm with it as if testing its perch, before moving the other one. It settled on her arm, but only for a second or two before flying away.

She watched in awe as its wings spread out over the tops of the trees. With just a small tip of its body, it turned through the air, gliding gracefully. So infatuated with him, she never heard the approaching footsteps behind her.

"The fact that you cannot hear or speak makes this almost too easy." A hand grasped her shoulder.

When she spun around, she found herself facing Euphemie, Ada, and another girl she didn't know. The three girls reached forward and grabbed her, pinning her and preventing her from running. "No one will ever hear you since you cannot speak or scream," Euphemie said. "Did you know there are several monks visiting? They love to take walks late at night, so we thought we'd give them a show. They may not be allowed to touch, but they can look, can they not?"

Rose fought and kicked with everything she had, but it was one person against three. They tossed her to the ground and tied her feet and hands with rope.

The third girl asked, "Why do you hate her so, Euphemie?"

"I don't know," Euphemie said. "But I do." She spat on Rose's chest as if to punctuate her remark.

Ada giggled and whispered, "Because she's so pretty and Euphemie's not."

Euphemie's expression closed down, and she punched Ada in the arm. "Close your mouth or you'll be next." The lass was distracted enough for Rose to get in one good kick, right in her crotch. Euphemie swore and said, "You'll regret that, bitch."

How Rose wished she could scream. She kicked and fought for all she was worth, even after they tied her legs together. She managed to sit up enough to butt Ada with her head. The lass reeled back and said, "Ow. Make her stop, Euphemie. She hurt me."

Euphemie reached for Rose's gown and cut it, then yanked it off of her, leaving her shivering in just her shift. "Och, look at those nice titties. I think the monks would love to see them up close." She grabbed Rose's shift and gripped her knife, ready to cut it off her when a bird flew down and squawked directly in her face.

"Leave, you rotten bird." She swung her arm out in an attempt to hit the bird, but he evaded her.

It was Rose's owl, come to help her. Its gold eyes flashed at her as it dived at the lasses who were attacking her. She felt her sire had sent her protection from beyond.

"I'm leaving," Ada said. "That owl is wild." She raced back toward the abbey and the third girl followed her, leaving Euphemie there by herself.

"Fine," Euphemie sneered. "Saved by an owl. I'll leave you with your shift, but I'll find you again. And if you tell anyone, you'll pay harder next time."

The owl squawked again, and Euphemie covered her face and bolted back down the path. Once the lasses had all fled, the owl landed in front of her body, strolling back and forth as if to judge if she were hale and hearty. It pecked at the gown on the ground next to her, tugging at a few strands, but then it stopped. Could it possibly be trying to cover her?

If so, he failed, but she knew she had a new friend.

She needed all the friends she could get.

Lying on the cold ground, tied up and unable to move, she forced herself not to cry.

Come what may, she would not allow anyone to hurt her anymore.

CHAPTER TWELVE

———◆———

TO RODDY'S SURPRISE, A GROUP of travelers arrived at Muir Castle early the next morn. Since he hadn't slept much, he made it to the gates before they dismounted.

Exhausted, Maggie said, "We tried to get here last night, but we were just too tired." Will helped Maggie down.

Gavin and Gregor came up behind them. "There must be more excitement here because there is naught to follow in the periphery other than the two abbeys. We're hoping you've found out more."

"Och, we've discovered plenty," Roddy said with a smirk, "but we're still short on details. We need to investigate more. We could use your help."

Cairstine and Braden came outside to greet them. "You must be famished. We have plenty of porridge. Come inside."

Steenie burst out the door, rushing down the steps of the hall. "We have visitors! And some people I don't know. The Wild Falconer is here! Did you hear that, Paddy? Where are your falcons, Will?"

Will whistled and the two birds appeared, swooping down near them to Steenie's delight. He did his best to chase each one when it neared him, but he failed.

Uncle Brodie emerged from the hall and muttered, "I wish I had half the lad's energy."

They made their way back to the hall, chattering amongst themselves.

Once the cousins finished eating, they all took a seat

around the largest table in the hall to share information.

"I take it you've also learned something?" Connor asked.

Will nodded. "Maggie's parents received word of one more group, in England. 'Tis the main artery of the network. It stays well hidden, and no one has any idea where 'tis located. In all likelihood, it moves around."

"Could it be related to the Englishmen we saw at the Abbey of Angels?" Roddy asked.

Will shrugged his shoulder. "Verra possible they are related. We shall keep that in mind as we continue."

"Shouldn't we go after them first?" Daniel asked. "Mayhap 'twould put a stop to the rest. And we seem to be waiting for something to happen here. There's been naught, as of yet. Are we not wasting our time?"

"Hold on. Hear me out," Will said, raising a hand. "It would seem the third group, in the western Highlands, has increased their activity. More than half a dozen lasses go down the firth each month. Families are traveling to the king to complain about their missing daughters."

"Then why have we not come upon that yet?" Connor asked.

"I think 'twill be happening soon. We need to gather our resources and expect some movement soon if they follow the previous patterns," Will replied.

"The clans suspect a nun or someone similar arranges for the sale of the lasses," Maggie said, "but no one can identify the woman involved. I suspect the mother abbess at Sona Abbey may be who we're looking for."

"Are you sure 'tis a religious person?" Roddy asked. He had another possibility in mind, a mother who was not fond of her daughter and had access to a firth, but he hoped for Rose's sake it wasn't true.

"Aye, lasses have gone missing from a few abbeys—the kirk will not allow the families to see them because they're in training—but people have grown suspicious. You won't be surprised to hear that many of the lasses were left at

Sona Abbey. We have orders from King Alexander to stop the sale of the lasses. He's received enough complaints that he's spoken with the religious community about it, but he wants our group to root out the source. He thinks we can be much quicker about it, and after the information you have just given us, I cannot disagree with him. We're close." Maggie glanced from face to face as if gauging whether they were all in agreement.

"So you see," Gavin said, "we really are all heading to the abbey."

Maggie said, "We need a place to sleep because 'tis a distance away. Do you have enough room for us, Braden? Will and I don't mind sleeping under the stars, but if the weather turns bad, we'd like the stables."

"Nonsense," Uncle Brodie said. "We have plenty of unused chambers inside Muir Castle. Cairstine's sire built a strong fortress, and from the sound of things, you may stir up some trouble in your travels, so 'twould be best if you're all behind a curtain wall. The four of them ran into a large group of reivers before they returned from their scouting. 'Tis most unusual in this area. Word must have gotten around that someone in the area is dealing in quite a bit of coin. I'll stay back with Steenie and Cairstine and Celestina. The rest of you need to move on this soon."

Maggie nodded. "Our thanks." Turning to Roddy, she asked, "And have you discovered anything? Any unusual activity at Rose's home?"

"Aye, indeed. Her mother just moved her to Sona Abbey," Roddy explained.

"What? Why?" Maggie asked

Connor did his best to hide his smirk. "She tells all that Rose will be taking her vows, but Rose says she was moved there for kissing a lad." His smirk could no longer be contained, and he tipped his head toward Roddy.

Gavin guffawed. "Roddy, you devil. You've sent a lass off to the abbey for teaching her bad things?"

"Laugh all you want about that part, but the truth of it is quite twisted." He then proceeded to tell them what Jean MacDole had told her daughter about sinning.

Silence descended on the group as they considered such cruelty.

Maggie whispered, "Tell me how you think this affects our mission."

Roddy said, "She got rid of her daughter because something illegal is going on at MacDole Castle. Rose already told us about the boat that visits the dock, and last night she indicated her mother may know something about it. What if she's tied to someone at the abbey?"

Connor nodded. "Aye, and if the operation became too large for them to rely solely on trading lasses from Sona Abbey, perhaps they started building Abbey of Angels to expand—and to keep people off their trail. They can send a constant supply of lasses there."

Will said, "I suggest we search the area in pairs today and on the morrow. I wish to know the area well before we form our plan to destroy their operation. I also don't want to make anyone suspicious that we're aware of their activities. If it weren't for the possibility of nabbing the Englishman, we could go after them right away, but we must proceed with caution. We wish to catch them in the act."

As the others discussed the journey to come, Roddy turned to Connor, "I need to travel back to Clan Grant before I go any further here. Do you have any reason to stop home?"

Connor gave him a probing look, but when he didn't rush to explain, his friend said, "I'd be glad to go with you. We can leave after we take our repast and still return in time to strategize."

Roddy nodded and set their proposal to Will and Maggie.

Maggie said, "Go. You know the area. We need to learn

it. You have time. From what we've learned from you and from our parents, this will not take place soon. We have time to prepare."

He could not handle another night of nightmares. It was time to find out the source of his dreams. If not, he'd never be confident in his ability to protect Rose.

It felt as though two days passed before she was discovered, though it was probably only an hour. At the sound of approaching footsteps down the path, she moved into the moonlight as much as possible.

She said a quick prayer that it was not Euphemie, and it was not.

Father Seward came upon her. "Rose?" he gasped in shock. "What are you doing out here? Are you hurt?" He untied her hands and feet, then grabbed the torn gown to cover her as best he could. "Who did this to you?" He helped her to her feet, but she struggled to stand, nearly tipping over, so he settled her on a nearby bench.

The hoot of her new friend echoed from above.

"Rose, I must know you are all right. Are you hurt anywhere?" His hands moved over her body, searching for injuries. He clucked when he saw the raw abrasions from the rope. "Oh my. I must get you to the infirmary right away. I care not what your mother says about leaving you in your chamber alone. Not after this."

Rose wanted to cry with relief. Perhaps Constance would find her way in to visit if she were in the infirmary. At least there, she would be able to wash away the filth, though mostly imaginary, of the attack.

"Can you walk, Rose?" He looked at her with such sympathy that she dared to hope she'd gained another ally. Would he go against her mother and allow her to learn to read?

She nodded, pulling the ripped garment around her for

privacy. Father Seward moved slowly beside her, making sure she could keep up with him.

They didn't pass anyone else along the way, but as soon as he entered the infirmary, one of the other nuns hurried to his side. "What happened? What's wrong with the poor lass?" They ushered her into the chamber she'd stayed in before, though the other bed was empty this time.

"She was attacked and bound. I don't think she was hurt, mayhap just roughly treated." He pointed to the abrasions on her wrists and ankles. "You must take care of these spots."

"Who did this to her?" the nun asked Father Seward.

"I don't know, but I aim to find out."

"Her mother will be furious." The nun brought both her hands up to her cheeks and shook her head with worry.

"No need to call her back just yet. Let's give it a few days. I want to find out who did this, investigate a bit more before we contact her mother. She'll want answers." He began to pace the small room.

Rose settled on the bed and hid under the plaid, resting her head down with a sigh. She was exhausted from the attack.

The nun looked at her and said, "Who did this? Was is a lad? A lass?"

Rose refused to answer. She would not tattle—she planned to take care of this herself.

"Was it Euphemie?"

Rose closed her eyes and didn't answer.

Father Seward spewed words of anger. "It could have been Euphemie or Ada or one of the other girls. Mayhap it was even one of the visiting monks. How will I find out if she cannot tell me? Shameful that she was stripped of her gown in a place of our Lord. Shameful. Give her a tonic to help her sleep if you must, Sister. She's to stay here one more day. In fact, I'll send her friend for a visit on the morrow, cheer her up a wee bit. Poor lass. Mayhap Constance can help me get through to her."

Once they left, Rose closed her eyes and allowed herself to think of Roddy Grant. How she wished he were here to comfort her. The thought of him had helped her get through the torment of the hour she'd spent bound on the garden path. Somehow she knew he would hold her, even allow her to cry if she needed it.

Roddy Grant made her believe there was more to life than climbing over rocks and listening to the sound of the waves crashing against the stones gleaming in the moonlight. And yet she couldn't deny that she missed the water. The force and power of the waves against the rocks had always given her strength.

Her happiest memories were of the time she and her father had spent on the cliffs over the water. Sometimes he would hold her hand and other times he would set her free to explore on her own, slipping here and there on the slick surfaces.

Only once had he admitted her mother did not understand the soul of a child, but he'd assured Rose her mother still loved her, just differently than he did. Her father had adored her, of that much she was certain. If her mother did indeed love her, it was a kind of love that baffled her.

She'd lost her father, but she'd never lose his love or the confidence his seeds of love had sown in her. Once he'd spoken to her about the day she'd meet a lad who would stir her differently than others did, and he'd advised to open her heart to him when that day came.

It was time to open her heart to Roddy. She prayed he'd return soon, and if he did, perhaps she'd have the courage to kiss him first this time. She needed Roddy.

And she also wanted to learn how to defend herself. She was sick of feeling like a helpless wee lassie, unable to do anything for herself. The time had come to take charge of her life.

CHAPTER THIRTEEN

IT WAS NEARLY DARK BY the time Roddy and Connor arrived at Clan Grant. They were greeted by Connor's older brothers, Jake and Jamie.

"You've missed me so that you've come to greet me?" Connor chided as soon as his brothers came abreast of them. "I take it you're desperate for my advice on how to run the lists?"

Jake said, "Och, we *could* use you in the lists. Jamie has been going soft ever since he married Gracie."

"I have every reason to be soft for a week or two," Jamie countered.

Roddy couldn't have been more surprised by this pronouncement, but Connor was quick to ask the question on his mind.

"And why would that be? I've not heard of you going soft before."

"Because Gracie is carrying, and my guess is 'tis a laddie." Roddy swore he saw Jamie's chest puff out a bit.

"Gracie?" Roddy asked. "Congratulations! I'm to be an uncle for a second time! I'll bet Aunt Maddie and my mother are quite pleased."

"Mama is especially pleased," Jake stated. "Kyla is also carrying. And if you wish to have some entertainment, watch Finlay and Jamie argue over who's going to have the first Grant laddie of the next generation."

Jamie snorted. "Och, Finlay likes to brag that Jake and I will only have lassies. He'd like to think he and Kyla will have the next laird of Clan Grant. After Jake and me, of course."

The banter continued until they passed through the gates and left their horses with the stable lads. It wasn't long before a voice called out to the group. Finlay's usual sarcasm carried across the courtyard.

"Jake and Jamie, why do you not go inside and practice your needlework with the lassies while I speak to the men about their travels. You'll need to learn quickly in order to teach your daughters."

Jamie said, "I'd be thrilled to have a wee lassie, but she'll have a brother before the next year is out, so do not get your hopes up, Finlay."

Appearing out of nowhere, Finlay crept up behind Jamie and crowed, "Kyla and I will have our second laddie before you have one, lad." He clasped Jamie's shoulder and said, "Someday, I'll give you pointers."

Kyla came out to the courtyard to greet them, emerging just in time to overhear her husband's boasting. "Please, Finlay. Enough bragging. You make me ill. Imagine how you'll feel when Aunt Caralyn announces in several moons that 'tis a wee lassie and she looks just like her grandpapa. My father wants another lassie, and I'm out to please him." Her eyes narrowed as she crossed her arms, glaring at her husband.

Finlay laughed and quickly amended his stance. "And you know I'd love a lassie who looks just like her mother as much as her grandpapa will." He wrapped an arm around her shoulders and kissed her on the cheek, only flinching slightly when she delivered an elbow to his side.

Roddy said, "Congratulations to both of you. Is my sire inside or is he at our cottage?"

"He left the keep about an hour ago," Jake said. "I'm sure he's home by now. You wish to speak with him?"

"Aye," he said. "Connor will fill you in on what we've learned. I'm going to grab a meat pie and head home for the night. I'll see you on the morrow."

Connor said, "We leave at first light?"

"Aye," Roddy replied, heading straight for the kitchens once they stepped into the empty great hall. "I'll see you then."

He wanted to speak with his sire alone and given the happy news about Jamie and Finlay's wives, he expected the men would be up late in front of the hearth.

He had a pair of violet eyes in his mind—but he would not be able to help Rose, or anyone, himself included, unless he faced his fears.

He cantered his horse at a good pace because the night was clear, and he loved galloping across the meadow between Grant Castle and the loch. All was dark inside their hut when it came into sight, but his sire sat out on the porch overlooking the loch in a wooden chair they'd built together.

"Roddy, I was not expecting to see you. What a pleasant surprise. The others are all asleep. Grab a goblet of ale and join me outside. 'Tis a beauteous eve."

"Thanks, Papa." He led his horse over to the loch for a drink, then took him inside their small stable for a nice meal of oats before he fetched his own drink from the hut. Sitting on the porch opposite his sire, he said, "I hear I'm to be an uncle. I hope Gracie's feeling well."

"She is. And you've heard the news about Kyla as well?"

"Aye. 'Twill be wondrous to have two at once. Which one will come first?"

"Your mama is not certain yet. She thinks Gracie, but they're verra close and you know the bairns make up their own mind about when they'll choose to arrive. A man can say all he wants, but nature rules all."

Roddy noticed how the lines around his sire's eyes were deepening, how age was beginning to creep up on him. He hadn't lost much of his golden hair, but it was turning a silvery white in places. He kept a trimmed beard of late, and his mother approved. Fortunately, he didn't have the physical problems that plagued Uncle Alex after his near miss with death, though his joints had started bothering him at times.

"Problems on your journey?" his father asked.

"Nay, Will and Maggie have found some information and we're to follow up on it. There is something I wish to ask you, though. I've been having a strange dream…a memory, mayhap…and Uncle Brodie suggested I speak with you."

His sire's only response was a brief lift of his eyebrows. "Go on."

Roddy decided to tell all. If he couldn't tell his father, who could he tell? When he'd been young and foolish, around ten and five or so, he'd thought his parents were ignorant, but he'd learned better. His father possessed a wisdom he only hoped to emulate someday.

"In the dream, I am in a pool of water and cannot rise to the surface. I always die in the end." He paused, then said in a gush, "I've been struggling with the fear of dying, and it's making me freeze up in combat. I don't know what to make of it, but Uncle Brodie said he recalled a time when I nearly drowned. I don't remember anything like that. Do you?"

"Aye, I recall it verra well." He cleared his throat, then paused for a moment, as if to collect his thoughts, before continuing. "You and Gracie were both underwater. She fell in and you went after her. I was just coming back from the lists when I heard the other bairns screaming, so I dove in after you. You don't recall it?"

"Nay," he rubbed his forehead as if it could force the memory to come forward, but to no avail. "Where in the loch?"

"Not far. Gracie had gotten caught in some netting, and you were trying to pull her out. Somehow you got caught in the same netting." His sire rubbed his beard, staring up at the stars for some time before he finished. "'Twas an old fisherman's net, not one of mine. Must have been there for years. Don't know why you never got caught in it before except it was quite deep. I freed you first and shoved you up to the surface. You must have been almost out of air because you kicked in a fury."

"And Gracie?"

"Gracie didn't fare so well. She was tangled pretty good. You, I just tugged out. I had to pull my knife out to cut her free. I saw her take her last breath. Watched her last bubble come out of her."

"What? You did?"

"I managed to grab her just as the fight left her. I feared we'd lost her. Your mother arrived just in time to see me drag her out of the loch."

"She'd stopped breathing?" How the hell could he have forgotten such an event?

"Aye. I carried her out and laid her on her side in the grass. Slapped her hard on her back a few times. She spewed quite a bit of water, but then your mother rolled her onto her belly and kept pushing on her back to get rid of the rest of the water. Gracie did not move much until she heaved all of her insides out."

"And she started breathing again?" He shook his head. "Aye, obviously, she's still here."

"After she heaved, she coughed and started breathing again, crying for your mother." His sire glanced at the glassy surface of the loch in front of them, the moon reflecting on the small ripples. "Scared the hell out of me. Never seen a lass heave so much. Thought she'd never stop. She took in quite a bit of water." He turned his head to glance at his son. "Did not seem to affect you much at the time. You weren't afraid to jump right back in the next day." A small grin started from one corner of his mouth. "Gracie didn't go back for over a fortnight. Scared the hell out of her."

"How old were we, Papa?" Maybe he'd been too young to recall.

He stroked his beard again before he spoke. "Must have been around your seventh summer because Gracie was just changing. Maybe around twelve. She remembers. If you see her before you leave, ask her. I think she'll be able to tell you more than I have."

He planned on it.

The next morn, he said his farewells before he headed up to the keep to meet with Connor. Thoughts of Gracie nearly dying had plagued him all night.

What would he have done without his dear sister?

Gracie had the heart of an angel. He didn't know anyone in Clan Grant who didn't think so. She'd always been an early riser, so he hoped she'd be up when he arrived at the hall.

He hurried up to the keep, careful not to bang the door loud enough to awaken anyone. The stone walls echoed every noise, especially when the hall was empty.

Thankfully, it was not quite empty this morn. Connor sat at one of the trestle tables with Uncle Alex and Jamie. He rushed over to them, barely able to contain himself. "Jamie, is Gracie up yet?"

"Good morn to you, too, cousin," Jamie said, winging his eyebrows up. "She's in the kitchens."

Roddy blushed and gave a hurried, "Good morn," to his uncle and Connor before heading off in search of Gracie.

He found her just inside the door to the kitchens. "There you are, Gracie. I'd hoped to see you before I left."

"Greetings to you, Roddy. How have your travels been?" She gave him the angelic smile they all knew so well, the same one that had driven all the lads in the clan daft.

"Fine, fine. We're having a successful mission, but I wished to congratulate you. I hear you and Jamie are going to make me an uncle."

She patted her belly, though it hadn't grown much yet. "Aye, we'll have a lad or a lassie in the spring, though please do not ask Jamie about it. He's quite obnoxious about it being a laddie."

"I'm happy for both of you." Roddy leaned in and kissed her cheek. "There's something I hoped to ask you about… I was talking with Papa last night. We sat out on the loch well into the night, chatting about when we were younger." How the hell could he abruptly ask if she remembered falling into the loch?

"We had many summer days on the loch, though you were in the water more than I was. 'Twas too cold for me many days."

"Papa mentioned something that troubled me. Do you recall the day we both nearly drowned?"

"Drowned?" She paused, drumming her fingers on her chin for a few moments. "Do you mean the time I heaved all that water up?"

"Aye." She was a wee bit older, but he couldn't believe she recalled the incident so easily. "Do you recall being under the water?"

"Hmm… Vaguely. I remember the netting. Why?"

Roddy wasn't quite sure how to answer her question, though this was Gracie, someone he trusted completely. "Have you ever had any dreams about it?"

Gracie clearly knew him better than he thought. She stared into his eyes and said, "Tell me all. You're holding back. What is this about dreams?"

"'Tis not important," he lied. "I've just had a couple of dreams about drowning in the loch. I'm sure you haven't had anything like that…"

"Nay." She sighed and leaned toward him, wrapping her arms around him for a hug. "Dear brother, stop torturing yourself about things that happened so long ago. I've had to. If you do, you'll be much happier."

Gracie would know the truth of that statement better than anyone. Her start in life had been far from pleasant.

Not wishing to bother her anymore, he said, "My thanks, Gracie. You always give good advice."

Now if he could only follow it.

CHAPTER FOURTEEN

———

SOMEONE KNOCKED ON THE DOOR of the sick chamber, then Constance crept inside just as Rose sat up. Seeing her dearest friend, she hopped out of bed and embraced the other girl, squeezing her hard. She gave her the sign they shared for "happy" to let her know how pleased she was to see her.

Only after the joy of seeing her wore off did Rose notice the troubled expression on Constance's face. "Oh, how I wish this had never happened to you," Constance mumbled. "I need to know exactly what happened. The tales they're telling in the hall are awful."

Rose took both her hands and sat cross-legged on the bed, indicating Constance should do the same.

She stared at her friend and teared up. "Your mother is horrible. She is the nastiest, meanest person ever. If she hadn't forced you to live alone, this never would have happened."

Rose shrugged, for she had no disagreement, and mouthed the words, "Tell me about stories."

"Tell you about the stories? Oh, I will. The story is they found you outside with naught on. The girls say the monks did it to you and they beat you, too, and now you're up here. Is it true?"

Rose shook her head. Through a process that was easier than their previous method of communication, Constance went through a multitude of guesses while Rose either nodded or shook her head. When she had the whole story, Constance scowled and said, "Euphemie is so cruel. Even so, I'm glad you're up here for a while. They wouldn't have let me visit you in your room. What are you going to do? They'll probably call that mean mother of yours."

Rose took her time conveying her message: she needed to see Roddy. When Constance finally guessed at her meaning, Rose asked her if she thought there was a way she could send a message to him.

Constance shook her head. "Nay, but I wouldn't worry about it. He kissed you. He'll be back."

Rose didn't know what to make of that statement and tipped her head, her latest method of telling her friend she didn't understand.

Constance giggled. "He likes you. He'll be back. 'Tis the way of lads. You'll see."

How Rose prayed she was right.

———◆———

Two nights later, Roddy stood in the trees outside the abbey glancing up at the tall structure, Connor and Daniel standing beside him. The group had been unsuccessful in learning anything about the Englishman because he'd disappeared. They'd traveled back to the new abbey, but it had been empty the day before. MacDole Castle was silent and there had been no activity on the sea loch, though they were all headed back for another patrol while Roddy's group returned to Sona Abbey.

Not knowing where else to go, they'd decided to return to Sona Abbey to see if anything had changed at the Abbey of Angels, and their only connection to that abbey was Rose and the novices in training. They'd first learned about the Abbey of Angels from one of the nuns serving meals.

"I have a bad feeling about this. I cannot explain it," Roddy said, his hands on his hips as he stood next to his horse.

"I'm glad to go with you," Daniel said. "I know exactly where her room is. I'll lead you there. Connor, you're on watch by yourself."

"Mayhap I'll sneak inside, too," Connor said, "I can make a different approach."

Daniel said, "Nay, we need someone outside to keep the horses ready. We could be on the run when we return. If what Maggie said is right, and someone here is connected with the Channel, they won't be happy to see anyone snooping around."

Roddy added, "There's naught going on elsewhere. There could be a meeting of sorts here about the Channel of Dubh, especially since it's due to have a new shipment. We must be careful. But I'm certain we'll learn something here. Connor and I agreed there was something odd about this place."

Connor added, "I didn't like the feeling between the abbess and the priest. I thought it could be the two of them at first, but they don't get along."

"Mayhap it's just one of them," Daniel said, raising eyebrows.

Roddy said, "The only person I suspect at the moment is Rose's mother, but she doesn't seem like someone who would sell girls. She has one of her own."

"That means naught," Daniel said. "She could sell others and keep her own."

Roddy said, "True. We're wasting time. The only way we'll find out anything is to get inside and speak with Rose or Constance."

Ten minutes later, Roddy and Daniel crept down the passageway where the novices slept, Daniel peeking in to each chamber, but they didn't find Rose. Daniel led the way down the hall to the room where he thought they might be. He motioned for Roddy to enter first.

As he crept into the dark chamber, Roddy's heart was beating so hard he thought it would rip a hole in his chest. What if another lass had been moved to this room? What if she screamed?

The lass sat up. To his relief, it was her friend, Constance.

She remembered him. Her voice whispered, "Roddy Grant?"

He whispered, "Aye. Where's Rose?"

"She's in the infirmary. I'll take you to her if I can."

"What happened?"

"She was attacked, but she wasn't hurt badly."

"I knew it," Roddy said bitterly, chastising himself for not coming back sooner. "Something in my gut told me something bad happened to her."

"Your gut was right. Poor Rose." She reached for his arm to still him, then said, "Before we go, I have something to tell you. Her mother came and has forbidden her to be around other lasses. She's kept in a chamber alone. It was because she was alone that she was attacked."

Roddy was stunned, but not surprised. If Lady MacDole were involved in the trade, she'd want to keep her daughter isolated to ensure she wasn't kidnapped. She'd also want to keep her ignorant of her part in this fiasco.

"Constance, I have a friend named Daniel outside. He'll help us get into the infirmary. I suspect 'twill be more difficult than getting on this floor.

"Follow me." The lass got up and grabbed her robe, so Roddy took the opportunity to open the door and tug Daniel inside.

"What is it?" He peered at the lass and asked, "Where's Rose?"

Roddy replied, "She's in the infirmary. This is her friend Constance."

Daniel asked her "Can you take us there?"

"Aye, but there's a problem. There are always nuns checking the rooms in the infirmary."

"Good, you lead us there," Daniel said at once. "Will you take her place in the bed? If you cover your head with the blankets and face the wall, the nun will think you're Rose sleeping. Just bury your head under the covers so they won't notice your red hair. Can you do that, lass? They need time to talk."

Constance whispered, "Aye, but what happened to your arm?" looking at his amputated arm from an accident in a swordfight when he was younger.

Daniel lifted his arm and glanced at it, then widened his eyes dramatically and said, "What's wrong with my arm? Och, where'd it go? My hand was here a minute ago. I swear it!"

Constance giggled and he shushed her with his other hand.

"Help us find Rose," he said, "and I'll explain it to you on another visit."

She nodded, doing her best to calm her laughter. "I can lead you to the infirmary, but how will we get inside? There are usually at least two nuns watching. One may be sleeping, but anything wakes them up."

Roddy looked to Daniel for ideas. His gaze narrowed, then his eyes popped open wider and a smile filled his face. "I know exactly what to do. Come with me and wait in the staircase. I'll run outside for a few moments and be back in a moment."

They made it to the staircase without being seen. The infirmary was on the third floor, so they had one more level to go up. Daniel disappeared then, leaving Constance and Roddy alone.

Roddy was desperate for more information about Rose. "So what happened to her? Can you not tell me? 'Twill be much quicker if you do."

Constance chewed on her lower lip, but finally said, "All right. She was attacked by a group of lasses. Three of them tied her up and took her gown, leaving her in just her shift. There were monks visiting at the time, and they hoped the monks would find her and embarrass her. The monks walk about at night."

"And who did find her?"

"Father Seward. He untied her and escorted her to the infirmary. He didn't want her to be left alone until he uncovered who was responsible for the nasty deed."

"And has he?"

"One of the girls squealed on the leader. I have not seen her about, so she is probably in the punishment cell. They have to stay alone for several days."

"Mayhap I'll have a word with her," Roddy said, an edge to his voice that he didn't even try to disguise.

"Nay, visit Rose first. She's anxious to speak with you. She needs to learn how to protect herself against those cruel bitches. Can you help her?"

A door closed, so they cut off their conversation and readied themselves to run up the staircase if need be, but Daniel's voice stopped them. "'Tis only me."

He climbed the staircase, and when he came up next to them, he whispered, "Allow me to go first. Where exactly do the nuns sit in the infirmary? I need to enter closest to them."

"Second door to the left down the passageway. They're just inside the entrance to the infirmary. There are several doors on the floor, mostly chambers for the nuns." She gave Daniel a puzzled look, likely wondering what he'd done and what he was planning, but Roddy didn't say a word. He trusted Ghost completely.

"Perfect," Daniel said, his eyes lit up as a grin spread across his face. Then he reached into his sporran and pulled out a wriggling mouse with his one hand.

"Do not scream," he cautioned Constance.

Constance's eyes widened, but she bit her lips and didn't cry out.

Daniel scoffed, "What's bothering you? 'Tis only a wee mouse."

Roddy said, "I think 'tis a bit big for a mouse."

Daniel advised, "This will work. I promise. Keep your eyes on the door, and when the two nuns run out, you must run in."

He left them alone for only a short time before the squealing began. Daniel waited until the nuns came out screaming and headed down the passageway before he swung the stairwell door open. "'Tis clear."

The nuns were far down the passageway still yelling when Roddy ushered Constance into the infirmary. They found Rose, who'd already left her room to explore the noise, apparently, as she was standing in the middle of the corridor, looking lost.

Roddy felt as though a bolt of lightning had struck him in the chest. He'd always remember this moment as being the one when he realized this lass meant more to him than any other, that there would be no forgetting Rose MacDole.

Rose stood in the middle of the corridor in her night rail, billowing in the breeze from the doorway behind him, which brought his attention to her every curve. Her dark hair fell almost to her hips in a sensuality that caught him by surprise. Her violet gaze caught his and the uncertainty and fear in them made him wish to wrap his arms around her and take all the pain away from her, protect her from the cruelty of the world.

More than anything, he wanted to make her his.

Forever. They'd be joined forever.

Another thought suddenly came to him. The ghost he and Connor had seen had looked almost exactly like Rose did in this moment. The only difference was in their hair color.

Constance grabbed Rose's hands and whispered, "Go. They did this for you. I'm going to sleep in your bed to cover for you." She gave her a quick squeeze and slipped into the chamber.

Roddy held his hand out, and Rose put hers in it without hesitation. He smiled and gave her a wee tug toward the door, pausing to peek out into the hall. Daniel yanked on it and said, "Go. They're getting assistance. I'll try to catch the wee rascal in case I'm in need of it again."

Roddy and Rose sailed down the stairway and out into the inky darkness of night, following the path through the trees and to the farthest edge of the property. When he finally stopped, he was panting and grinning. He spun on his heel to face her and wrapped his arms around her, sweeping her up off her feet.

He set her down and cupped her face. "You are hale?" he whispered.

She nodded, then tugged him down for a kiss. He growled with delight when his lips met hers. She parted for him and he slanted his head so he could devour her, stroking her tongue with a need he hadn't know was there until a few moments ago. Hellfire, their time together was short, so he needed to let her know how much it meant to him. He ran his hands down her sides, across the soft curves of her hips to her backside, caressing her until he could no longer stand to be apart from her. Then he molded her curves against him, their tongues dueling until they were both panting. He pulled back, his breaths raspy from their interlude, but something caught his eye on her tender skin.

When Roddy noticed the raw marks on his wrist, he dropped his hands from her face and reached for her hand.

She held both wrists up for him to see. They were raw from the rope, but his finger grazed a spot on one wrist because he thought he saw something else there.

He was right. There was a fresh wound, aye, but there was also a scar from a previous wound. Her mother had mistreated her grievously. A fury built inside his belly that fought to be released, but he tamped it down, reminding himself that losing his temper would not help her now. Reaching into his boot, he pulled out a dagger and held it up for her to see. "Constance told me you wish to learn how to protect yourself. I will teach you how to use this so you won't be taken advantage of again."

She nodded vigorously and ran her fingers down the side of his face. A noise came from behind him and he jumped up, spinning around with his dagger in his hand, but it was just an owl. It swooped down too close, closer than a normal bird would fly at night. He didn't try to hurt it, instead waiting to see what the creature would do next.

He tucked Rose behind him to protect her, and the bird responded with a loud hoot before settling on a low branch not far away. "What the hell?" he whispered.

Rose grabbed his wrist that held the knife, shaking her head as she stepped next to him. She mouthed the word, "Friend," and reached for the bird as if to pet it.

"He's your friend?" He glanced at her to make sure he'd understood her correctly, then stared at the bird of prey again, well-known for the power in its fierce talons.

She nodded and tried to explain more, but he only took away a few words. From what he could discern, she was telling him the bird was her protector. He stood and faced the feathered creature, its gold eyes eerily locked on his. "So you are the lass's protector, my friend?"

There was no denying he'd heard of stranger things.

The owl edged down the branch and then back again. It lifted his chin and said, "Hoo."

"Are you trying to tell me what to do? You wish for me to teach your lass how to protect herself?"

The owl repeated, "Hoo."

Rose reached for Roddy's chin to force him to look at her. She pointed to him, then her, and placed her hands on either side of her head, tipping it back and forth.

"Daft? You think I would consider you daft because you befriended an owl?" He couldn't help but grin. "Nay, lass, you are far from daft. Animals befriend people all the time. My cousin's lad has a pony who uses his hind legs against anyone who'd try to hurt him. The lad thinks he's his best friend. I don't come between them."

Rose had a way of shaping her hand just so whenever

she meant to say "good" or "aye." She had a way of making herself understood. The way she'd overcome the difficulties she faced moved him, and a surge of protectiveness almost choked him. He reached for her and clasped her hand. "Come. Let's make your friend happy."

He opened her hand and placed the hilt of a dagger on her palm, closing her fingertips around it. "If you wish to kill a person, the best place to strike is right across the vessel in their neck. The blood comes out fast and powerful and they'll die in minutes." He demonstrated how she could make the slash.

"But you may not wish to kill your attacker, especially if 'tis a lass from the abbey, but there are many other places you can attack them. If someone is on top of you, you can stab them right here in their lower back." Giving her his back, he demonstrated exactly where she should aim her weapon.

He continued his lesson, showing her how to put her body behind a swing to give herself more force. He also gave her a brief lesson on how to hurt a man by kicking him in the bollocks.

The owl squawked and lifted his wings as if in approval. The bird's behavior was uncanny, intelligent—and he seemed desperately concerned for Rose's well-being. He remembered hearing one of his aunts speak about owls and their unique connection to the spiritual world...

Roddy looked at her and said, "You lost your father, did you not?"

She nodded her head in agreement, her eyes filled with sadness.

"Rose," he said softly, "I think he may have sent this owl to look after you." He strode over to the owl in the upper branches of the tree and motioned for the bird to come closer. To his surprise, it dropped to the branch directly in front of him.

The memory of the ghost he and Connor had seen at

the guest house in the abbey flashed through his mind again, reminding him that at least one spirit was interested in protecting her. He glanced over his shoulder at the innocent lass standing behind him.

Had Rose been so mistreated that the powers above had sent a ghost to help her, and now an owl? A shiver ran down his spine, but he knew enough not to ignore these types of signs.

He stared into the golden eyes as a memory stirred him. "'Twas you, was it not? You were the owl who flew in my path when I left the abbey before. Never mind. You need not answer. You were trying to get my attention, give me a message that I was needed here. I've heard your message, friend of Rose. I'll not ignore you again."

No. He would heed the messages he'd received, both from the owl and the apparition. Roddy said, "I'll protect Rose as much as I can, but you need to keep watch over her for a wee bit longer, until I can return with more warriors. Agreed?"

The bird unfolded his wide wings before tucking them back into his sides. It uttered a soft, "Hoo."

"Good." He returned to Rose and said, "You must find a way to hide the dagger. You can sew a pocket into your gown or find boots you can tuck it into."

She nodded, indicating she understood.

"I have a few questions for you, then I must go." He led her back to the bench, underneath the owl's perch. When she sat down, he lifted her and settled her onto his lap.

The owl moved two steps closer.

Roddy lifted his gaze to the golden eyes and said, "Don't worry. I respect her."

Rose giggled and leaned her head against Roddy's chest.

He settled one hand on her hip and the other behind her neck, massaging her lightly. "When I was here before, you tried to tell me something about your mother and the boat. Could it have been carrying people? Young people?

Lassies?"

She nodded vehemently, but then thought for a moment before she started silently babbling, mouthing words to explain what she saw.

It struck him, not for the first time, that she didn't act like a lass who'd never spoken before. Something about her past didn't seem to fit. "Rose, did you speak when you were young?

She gave him a strange look as if she didn't understand, or did she? Was she trying to hide something? Was she ashamed of something in her past?

He gripped her chin softly and said, "Will you show me your tongue?"

She did. He was stunned, but he'd been correct in what he thought he'd seen.

And what he thought he'd felt earlier.

"Rose," he whispered, "What happened to the tip of your tongue?"

CHAPTER FIFTEEN

R OSE REACTED SO STRONGLY SHE didn't know what to make of her own actions. She bolted from Roddy's lap, swinging her arms as if she wished for him to leave her alone. To go far, far away.

What was he talking about? What was wrong with the tip of her tongue?

Visions of someone screaming and hollering filled her head—her, it had been her—and the pain...oh, the pain. She had no idea how to stop the memories from cascading through her. Spinning in a circle, she clutched her hands to her head, wishing to stop her brain's spinning.

"Rose! Rose!" Roddy cried, wrapping his arms around her from behind, whispering in her ear. "Rose, come back to me, please?"

His voice centered her. She grabbed his hands as if they would anchor her to the present. She gasped for breath, her entire body convulsing with a fear unlike any she'd ever experienced. "Rose, I'm here. I'll not leave you like this."

His sincerity, his honesty, it soothed her soul. Tears covered her cheeks and she let herself collapse against this man who held her, who promised to help her.

As soon as she gave up fighting, he said, "I don't know what happened, but whatever it is, I'll help you." He sat on the bench and settled her on his lap again. The owl was pacing its branch, making anxious sounds, but Roddy had eyes only for her. "Did you have an accident when you were younger? Or...Rose, did your mother do this to you?"

She shook her head in disbelief, quite simply because she couldn't remember any such thing. She didn't understand all the flashes of memories that had erupted within her, as destructive and burning as flames peeling her skin.

She wept against Roddy's chest, and he simply held her, his arms sure and strong. She hadn't felt so comforted, so *heard*, in a long time.

Stroking her hair, he said, "Do you remember what I told you about my fear of death? I just found out something happened to me when I was young—something I don't remember at all. The nightmares I've had of late… they all end with drowning. I'd wake up covered in sweat, gasping for air, fighting to breathe. I had no idea why.

"Then I spoke of the dreams with my uncle and my sire, and they told me I'd nearly drowned when I was younger. I jumped into the loch after my sister, and we were both caught in an old fishing net. My sire had to cut us both out. I still don't recall the incident, but somehow it's been playing over and over again in my sleep. Mayhap 'tis something like that."

She calmed, considering his words, wondering if there could be truth to his tale. Could something have happened to her when she was younger? Something so awful she'd forgotten it? She glanced at the owl, meeting its golden gaze. What did it mean?

A voice she recognized but could not place carried to them from over the wall.

"We need to move. There are horses headed this way."

Roddy glanced at the wall. "I'll be right back, Connor," he said. "Going to get her inside." Then he shifted his gaze to her and planted a kiss on her forehead. "My cousin has been watching the periphery. Come, we must return. I promise I'll come back for you. We must find Daniel."

She took the dagger and clutched it close to her chest as she followed him. Her mind was still full of disjointed thoughts and memories, so she sucked in a breath and forced herself to instead focus on Roddy, how it felt to be close to him, to take in his scent of the woods and the outdoors. She did her best to lock them in her memory so she could return to them when she needed it most.

Roddy knocked on the door close to the stairwell, and Daniel swung it open at once. "Hurry. I found another critter, but this is one is a rabbit. They may not be as quick to run from something so cute."

A few moments later, she was back in the infirmary, Daniel hurrying Constance away to her room. Roddy gave her one final kiss on the lips, a soft sensual kiss that nearly left her breathless. "You believe me?" he asked, whispering carefully, desperate to be certain she understood him. "I'll be back with others. We'll find out what is happening here. Use your knife if you must."

She nodded, wanting to hold on to him forever.

Roddy was everything to her.

———◆———

The group reconvened at Muir Castle. They gathered around one of the trestle tables while Roddy shared what he'd learned from Rose. It wasn't much, but his questions had upset her, and he'd needed to teach her how to protect herself.

Maggie patted his shoulder. "Don't trouble yourself. We can sneak in to speak with her if need be. You did what was necessary."

Roddy added, "Since most of you believe in Paddy the Pony, Steenie's friend, I'll share with you that Rose seems to have an owl that has become her protector. I know it sounds unusual, but try looking a golden-eyed owl in the face and arguing with it while its talons move back and forth across a thick branch. It made a believer of me. Rose says it's her friend."

Maggie said, "I believe every bit of that."

"I'll not argue with you," Gregor said.

Braden snorted. "Anyone who doesn't believe it could happen, go try talking to Paddy the Pony."

Connor asked, "What did the rest of you find?"

Maggie said, "Will and I searched out the Abbey of Angels and we found it without any difficulty. I'd say there were less than ten living or working there this day. There's still evidence of carpentry there. What bothers me most is that no one outside of Sona Abbey seems to have heard of an abbey in that area. I doubt Abbey of Angels, if that's the true name, has any connection to the church."

"We found the dock at the sea loch," Gavin said, "There's a clearing nearby that looks as if it's been used for tents before. No evidence of recent usage. There could be something coming soon."

Maggie put a hand to her head, as if struck by a sudden pain, then rested her head down on her arms. The motions reminded him of the headaches her sister suffered whenever she had one of her visions. Added to the other strange things he'd experienced of late, the spirits and the owl, it made him uneasy.

Roddy turned to Will, arching his brow as if to ask, "Is she hale?"

Will sighed. "Ever since we moved higher into the Highlands, Maggie has had a headache and it continues to worsen."

Roddy glanced at her. "Anything I can do to help?"

"Gavin, Maggie, and I will return to the Abbey of Angels on the morrow, and you, Connor, and Daniel will return to Sona Abbey. We need to find out who's in charge. And we need to know who, specifically, travels between the abbeys. I hate to send you on patrol again, but until the day comes when they move, that's the best we can do."

"Is Maggie well enough to go along?" Connor asked.

Gavin joined them. "Maggie's never had Molly's ability as a seer before, so we don't know what to expect."

"Something powerful must be at work here," Will said.

The group stood silent for a moment.

"Ready yourselves," Will said. "We'll leave tomorrow eve so we arrive when the abbeys are a bit quieter. I'll do my best to help Maggie in the meantime. Get some rest. One of these nights, we'll be up for the duration after they make their move. Braden has said he'll join us if Maggie is not hale enough."

Will moved over to his wife. "I need to get Maggie back to our chamber." He swept her up in his arms and climbed the stairs, ignoring her weak protests, and Gavin trailed along behind them.

When the others were out of hearing, Roddy turned to Connor. "Come to the stables with me?"

The suggestion seemed to confuse him, but he nodded and followed Roddy outside.

"What's at the stables?"

"I'll explain as soon as we're inside."

No one looked to be around, but when they moved toward the stable, a wee lad flew by them, wide-eyed and frantic.

"Steenie?" Roddy yelled. "Is something wrong?"

The laddie stopped to answer him. "Nay, but Mama said I must feed my pony before I can eat."

On a whim, he asked, "Is Paddy acting normally?"

Steenie had already taken off at a run toward the keep, but he slowed enough to explain what he'd seen. "Nay, he's daft today. 'Tis why I'm leaving. He kept nudging me, and then he shook his whole mane and pushed me against the wall. He's never done that before. I think he wanted me to leave. He scared me."

Roddy and Connor exchanged a look. Roddy murmured, "Or mayhap he wished for you to find someone."

"Well, I found you. Go make my pony happy. Please?" He whirled around and ran toward the keep.

Connor's furrowed brow told him he still didn't understand what Roddy was leading him to.

"You'll see."

When they opened the door to the stable, they were surprised to hear the racket coming from the last stall. There were only five stalls, but whatever animal was in the last one was stirring up the straw and making his discontent known.

Could it be Paddy?

Roddy and Connor made their way to the end, passing the large warhorses and two mares before stopping at the last stall. Paddy pawed the ground and gave a high-pitched neigh as if he'd been sent out in a storm without rider.

"Calm down, laddie," Connor said, reaching over the gate to attempt to pat his head, but Paddy wasn't about to take it. He snorted at them both, then sighed as if to tell them to get on with whatever they were there for.

Roddy whispered, "Connor, I'm going to ask you not to repeat what I'm about to say."

"All right, but why are you whispering?" Connor's hands were on his hips as if he were questioning his cousin's soundness of mind.

"Because I don't want anyone else to overhear us, mostly because I'm not sure whether I believe it myself."

"Believe what?" Connor asked, though his tone told Roddy he was thinking of the apparitions from the abbey.

"Don't you see? The apparition you'd rather not think about from the abbey told us we had to help 'her'. Second, Maggie, who's sister to a seer, has a huge headache. Third, Rose is watched over and protected by an owl, and last but not least, Paddy is restless and unsettled. This is all about Rose. Something really bad is happening at the abbey."

Paddy let out a loud sigh as if to say, "Finally, someone understands."

Connor took two steps back from the pony, his eyes wide. "I don't know what you're talking about. We all know what's likely happening at the abbey, and I got a bad feeling about the place, too, so I won't disagree with you there. But suggesting spirits and ghosts are involved? Nay. I'll not go along with that." Paddy finally shifted his stare from Roddy to Connor, who quickly declared, "And what the hell does that horse have to do with all this?"

Roddy groaned and said, "If you don't believe there's some old spirit guiding that wee beast who's protecting Steenie, then you need to think again. A spirit sent that owl to protect Rose, too. I'm sure of it. Now tell me what you recall of the ghost we saw, and I'll be quiet."

His cousin used the tip of his boot to push the straw and dirt in circles in the middle of the stable, then moved down to the stable to where his warhorse was chewing on oats. His horse nickered and came over to greet him, and all Connor could do was lean his head on his horse's withers, rub his mane, and close his eyes.

Roddy didn't know what to say, so he allowed the two the moment together. A man and his horse shared a power-ful bond, and he knew what he was suggesting was beyond believable, especially for someone as anchored in reality as Connor had always been.

A few moments later, his cousin whispered, "She said we must help her when she arrives."

Roddy nodded, "Rose. She meant Rose. The ghost was sent to us to get help for an innocent lass. And if we don't heed her message and get Rose away from the abbey, there will be more than wildly flying owls, moody ponies, and headaches."

Paddy went back to his oats with a deep sigh.

Connor whispered, "You're right. We'll help her. But keep that pony away from me. He scares me, too."

Paddy snorted.

CHAPTER SIXTEEN

R OSE SLEPT IN LATE THE next morn, but she bolted up when the door opened. An embarrassed Father Seward stared back at her. He quickly closed the door again, so she covered her legs with her night rail before he opened the door the second time.

Father Seward stood there, a small smile on his face. "Rose, you've slept in, I see. If you please, would you find your way to my office in a quarter of an hour? I need to speak with you."

She pretended not to understand everything, so Sister Murreall, who'd come up behind him, did her best to relay the message with her hands and fingers.

Rose nodded, then pointed to the urn and basin.

Father Seward hastily closed the door, so she started her ablutions, doing her best to be timely, but she felt as if she were moving in slow motion. She reviewed everything she'd discussed with Roddy, even all the moves he'd taught her. She checked to make sure the dagger was still completely concealed beneath the stand the urn sat on. As soon as she had the opportunity, she'd sew a pocket in her gown as Roddy had suggested.

When she was ready, she made her way toward Father Seward's office on the first floor. The blood in her veins roared to life, pounding fear into her heart—why was she being summoned? What was to happen now?—but she forced herself to stay the course.

She didn't see anyone, though she moved through the great hall. No students were around, for this was their normal time for chores. Each student was assigned to work in the abbey in some way or another.

She knocked on the door, and Father Seward swung the door open. The look on his face was far more pleasant than she'd expected. What was this about? An uneasiness crept up her neck. He gestured for her to take the seat in front of the desk, then closed the door.

"Rose, I'm glad you were able to rest this morn. I wished to let you know the decision I've made. I am going to allow Constance to return to your chamber. I do not wish for you to be alone. You cannot hear when someone approaches you, so I'm sure those nasty lasses took you by surprise." He paused for a moment and peered at her from across the desk. "Am I speaking too quickly for you to read my lips? You…may…stay…with…Constance."

She watched his lips, then let the big smile she'd been holding back spread across her face when he repeated his news.

"Now, I know who did this to you. Ada came forward and told us everything. Since she confessed, she'll not be punished as severely as the other two. I know it was all Euphemie's idea."

She didn't react in any way, so he leaned closer and said, "Euphemie. Punished." Then, as if it were an added thought, he said, "Euphemie did this to you, is that not correct?"

Rose stared at her hands and nodded.

"As I suspected. I will send a message to your mother."

Rose fought with every bit of self-control she had not to react strongly to his words. This would not go well.

"Never mind. I'll handle your mother. She'll no longer tell me how to handle my affairs. Leaving you alone like that was a travesty, and 'twill not happen again." He moved to the door and opened it, peeking out into the corridor. "Constance, my dear, please take Rose back to her chamber. You'll be staying with her again. I'm sure you heard about her attack. If you hear any strange noises in the middle of the night, you are to notify one of the night guards immediately. Is that understood?"

"Aye, Father," Constance replied. Rose could see how happy her friend was about being returned to her chamber. "If I may be so bold, may I continue her reading lessons?"

Father Seward frowned and pulled on his chin for a moment, then said, "I don't see why not. The lass should have something positive in her life. I'll speak with her mother. Now, carry on, lasses."

The two of them left the great hall and headed toward their chamber. As soon as they reached it, they hurried inside, closed the door behind them, and hugged each other while Constance squealed enough for the both of them.

———————◆———————

Roddy fell asleep dreaming of a pair of violet eyes. After spending most of the previous night awake, he needed rest before they returned to the abbey the next night. When they did, he hoped to see her, though he guessed she would no longer be in the infirmary. Her wounds had not been severe.

He slept fitfully, but then awakened in a sweat. He'd had the nightmare again, but it had been different this time. This time, he remembered.

In the dream, he watched Gracie go flying off the end of the dock. She went under the surface and didn't come right up. Ashlyn stood behind him and screamed, "Mama! Roddy, do something!"

Roddy dove in because Ashlyn had not been a strong swimmer at the time. He felt around for Gracie but didn't find her. He went up for air once, and all he could hear was Ashlyn's terrified screams, so he dove down again. This time he went much deeper, and he hit flesh.

He remembered feeling Gracie's arm. She was flailing

about, so he grabbed one of her hands and tugged on it, but she didn't move. He reached for the other, only to find himself snagged in the same tangle of netting that held her captive. Gracie yanked him closer so she could hug him, then he couldn't set himself free.

Every thought came in slow motion: the memory of feeling powerless, of flailing limbs, of wanting to scream at the top of his lungs, of praying someone would save them both.

In that moment, he'd known that he was about to die. The fear felt as raw as it had that day.

The dream ended as the memory did—with the strong arm of his father pushing him up toward the surface.

Roddy hadn't died, and neither had Gracie.

Wiping the sweat from his brow, he realized he was panting as if he were still underneath the water, even though he was nowhere near it.

He remembered everything—the fear, the helplessness, the darkness. Perhaps his fear of dying would be over now that he'd confronted it.

Perhaps his nightmares would finally end.

———◆———

Rose and Constance tiptoed down the stairs in the middle of the next night, heading deep down into the underbelly of the abbey—the cellars.

The cellars held barrels of ale, vegetables, and many other treasures.

But it was also where those who were being punished stayed. They were kept in the cold until God, and the abbess, forgave them their sins.

Rose had painstakingly communicated Roddy's message—that they were to find out all they could about the abbey. She'd convinced her friend that they had no time to waste because lassies' lives could be at stake. They'd agreed to wander around the abbey at night and see what they could learn. So off they'd gone on their mission as soon as the sun dropped. Constance had even spoken to a young guard, who'd been all too glad to show off his knowledge of the abbey, revealing the number of guards they had, and the number of nuns.

They'd been unable to discover the identity of the wealthy benefactor, though Constance suspected it could be Rose's mother. Rose was not as convinced—though she'd heard Father Seward discuss a payment with her mother, she'd never had any knowledge of their wealth.

For the last bit of their exploration, they'd gone here, to the cellars. According to Constance, one of the other lasses had snuck down here the night before to see Euphemie. Apparently, six of the chambers were occupied, all with lasses being punished. She could have simply told Roddy as such, but she thought it best if they verified it first.

Rose's heart beat so hard it echoed in her ears as they approached the small chambers clustered at one end of the cellars. She moved up to the first of the doors, finally daring to peek inside the embedded window, and then spun around to face Constance.

The chamber was empty.

They quickly checked the rest of the chambers, only to find they were empty, too.

Constance grabbed Rose's hand. "Where did they all go?" she asked.

Rose had her suspicions, but she needed confirmation. She pointed toward the exit, then tugged her friend toward it.

After much searching, they located the guard with the wagging tongue, the one who'd given Constance all the information before.

"I heard that someone was punished for attacking my friend." Constance said.

The guard nodded importantly. "Aye, she was punished, but she and her friend have been moved. You'll not see them again, so your friend needn't worry."

"Oh," Constance said, "I wished to tell her what I think of her. Poor Rose. What a terrible experience she suffered through, and nary a guard saw the whole episode. Where were you when it happened?"

The guard's smile disappeared, and he narrowed his gaze at Constance. "You'll never get the opportunity to talk with her. Judge her if you wish, but do not judge us guards. We're ordered to do far more than you would ever guess."

Constance batted her eyelashes at him, letting her gaze linger on his arms as if in admiration. "What kind of things? I cannot even imagine."

Rose did her best not to smile at Constance's performance.

"Sometimes we must travel to a neighboring abbey. We have chores you have no idea about and never will." He crossed his arms and glared down his long nose at Constance. "'Tis not easy."

Constance wasn't easily intimidated. "Neighboring abbey? What abbey is that?"

"I was informed this was a plan of Father Seward and Mother Abbess. They were given a large amount of coin to build this abbey. They turned the ruins of a castle into a beautiful place, but the king does not... Never you mind. 'Tis not for young lassies to know."

"But where is it?"

"Southwest. The king has not named it, but they call it Abbey for Angels. 'Twill hold many novices in the future, but Father has already sent a few lasses there."

Rose had to find Roddy.

CHAPTER SEVENTEEN

———◆———

AFTER MUCH DISCUSSION, IT WAS decided Maggie would stay at Muir Castle. Braden and Gregor would instead accompany Will on the journey back to the second abbey. Gavin was to join Roddy's group—while Will and Braden could possibly find naught for their efforts, they *knew* Sona Abbey was dangerous. It made sense to send the larger group there. Roddy would try his best to get Rose away from the abbey so she could show them the area around her castle. He managed to convince the rest of them that Rose could help them if she were with them. It was possible the cave held more than he'd seen, so it was worth exploring. He'd been able to do it without mentioning the ghost he and Connor had seen.

Once they finished their separate missions, they were to meet near MacDole Castle.

Before they left, Maggie called them to her. She sat in a chair in front of the hearth, kneading her forehead. "This headache keeps worsening," she said, "and I've been having dreams are about ships and lassies, so I fear we cannot wait any longer."

No one said anything.

"Then Godspeed to all of you. I shall remain here with Cairstine, Aunt Celestina, and Uncle Brodie. If we receive any more messages, either Uncle Brodie or I will contact you."

Their instructions clear, they moved as a group to the stables, a wee lad skipping behind them.

Steenie caught up with Will, known to the lad as the

Wild Falconer. "Are you taking your falcons with you? Which one is faster? Which one is meaner? See how fast I can be." He raised his arms out like the wings of a bird, flying around the courtyard and pretending to dive and hunt.

"Like this, Falconer?" the lad pressed.

Roddy couldn't help but smile. Steenie was so fond of Will's birds of prey, he'd taken to dropping Will's name and just calling him Falconer.

"Look! Here come your falcons. I see them." He jumped up and down as he stared up at the sky, his gaze tracking the peregrine and then the smaller merlin. "Will they attack? Are you taking them?"

Braden strolled over next to Steenie and put his arm around him. "Now, I know you love Will and his falcons, but don't pester him too much. They'll go with us on every mission, I expect."

Steenie stopped in his tracks, his lower lip protruding. "But I love them. Can I not follow them when they're here?"

Braden glanced at Will, who didn't seem to be bothered by the lad. "Of course you can. Ask your questions."

Will always waited for Steenie to get his questions out before he answered, likely because it would be fruitless to interrupt the lad. When Steenie finally ran out of words, Will said, "They go wherever I go, Steenie. 'Tis your job to stay and protect the women. Protect your mama and cousin Maggie. She does not feel well. You have a big job to do."

Steenie's chest puffed out. "I'll do a fine job. I'll help you with the horses. Paddy likes to pretend he's big like Grandpapa's horse, but he cannot go with you."

The lad raced ahead of them to the stables, so Connor took the opportunity to describe the clearing not far from MacDole Castle where he and Roddy had met before. It would suit their purposes well.

Roddy's group headed out several minutes later. They

didn't chat much until they arrived on the outskirts of Sona Abbey. It was nearly midnight, but they had enough time to get inside and then make their way toward the meeting place at MacDole Castle.

"Shall I sneak in like last time?" Daniel asked Roddy.

"You trust him to go with you?" Gavin scoffed. "He's a jester, not serious enough. I'm the best at sneaking about and getting results." His wide grin told everyone exactly who the jester was.

Connor laughed. "You must have heard about all the lasses here training to be nuns. You just wish to sneak inside to peek at them."

Gavin's shocked expression didn't fool any of them. They were all used to the antics of Gavin and Daniel both. The two loved to bounce boasts and jests off each other, much to the amusement of all the cousins.

"Jest with him all you like once I have Rose out safely," Roddy said. "Until then, you're out here with your bow."

Gavin grumbled, but not too much because he knew his reputation of being one of the top archers in all the land rivaled his mother and his sister. His goal was to gain the title from both of them someday, but that day hadn't arrived yet.

Once Connor and Gavin were in place, Daniel and Roddy followed the curtain wall to the fence around the back, then shimmied over the wrought-iron barrier as they'd done before.

"Shite, guards ahead," Daniel whispered, motioning for Roddy to stay low.

"Where?" Roddy turned his head to search to the right of their location, but Daniel shot off to the left. Moments later, Roddy heard the moan of a man knocked out by Daniel. "What the hell? How did you see him?" Hellfire, but Daniel was talented.

Daniel, serious for once, replied, "I didn't see him. I felt him." Then he pointed off to the side and disappeared before Roddy could ask him what exactly he'd seen.

Another thump told him Daniel had taken out another guard with a blow to his head. He returned in a matter of seconds. "Felt him, too."

"And now?" Roddy whispered.

"We're free to move."

They'd almost made it to the back entrance to the abbey when Daniel held his hand up to indicate that Roddy needed to halt.

"The lasses," he said, nodding.

Sure enough, Rose and Constance appeared in the dim moonlight, creeping about just as they were.

Roddy stepped out of their hiding spot, not far from them. As soon as she saw him, Rose raced toward him and leapt into his arms, wrapping her arms around him. Constance followed behind her. "We could be in trouble," she said. "The guards are looking for us. We were sneaking around in the cellars last night and tried again this night, but I think they've discovered us."

Roddy set Rose down, though he held on to her hand. "I'm taking you far away from here. I don't like all that has happened. I'm also hoping you can show us your cave and all the paths that lead away from it. There has to be a place where the boats dock. It could be the physical dock we've seen, but is there a place inside where they could be hidden?"

Rose nodded.

"Constance, would you like to come with us?"

She nodded furiously, pulling her mantle more tightly around her. "Whatever they're doing here, it isn't right."

"Daniel, protect her and help her over the fence." Daniel bent over at the waist and held his arm out as if to escort her to a regal ball. Constance giggled.

"Hush, you two," Roddy said, but he couldn't help but smile. Daniel did know how to lighten a moment.

A few moments later, they had just gone over the fence

when the shout of a guard brought all the attention down on them. He'd known there were about thirty guards about the abbey, but this was the first time they'd seen more than two. Suddenly ten appeared out of nowhere.

They raced to the front of the abbey, ducking in and around any shrubbery they could. Connor and Gavin were both on horseback, Connor with his sword drawn and Gavin ready with his bow, and they'd prepared the two other horses to leave.

"Go," Connor said. "We'll cover you both. Get the lasses away from here."

Roddy didn't wait. He lifted Rose onto his horse and mounted behind her, sending his loyal warhorse away from the abbey with a neigh and a snort, proof that the beast loved a challenge. Daniel and Constance were directly behind them. He charged ahead without looking back for possible pursuers, taking the path that headed directly toward the loch and MacDole Castle.

Once they were a good distance away and Connor and Gavin caught up with them, Roddy slowed his horse to a canter.

Gavin pulled his horse abreast of Roddy's while Connor and Daniel rode ahead of them. Constance appeared to be sound asleep in front of Daniel. Winking at Roddy, Gavin said, "Now I see why you've become such a religious man, cousin. She's quite a beauty."

Roddy rested his hand on Rose's waist. "Do you always say things like that in front of the women you help?"

Gavin shrugged his shoulders as he glanced at Rose first, then Roddy. "What? You said she's deaf. If she cannot hear me, I cannot hurt her feelings. Besides, what's wrong with saying the truth? She is beautiful."

Daniel spun around with a grin, one Roddy understood but Gavin didn't. "What else would you say about the lass?"

Gavin said, "I don't know." His eyes narrowed at Daniel. "I could say lots of things, I suppose, but you first, cousin."

He'd caught on to the fact that there was a trick—though not what the trick was. Daniel saw the full picture, so he knew how best to respond. "I think she's highly intelligent." He gave Rose a nod of encouragement.

"Well, I think she's probably got a nice arse," Gavin said, "but I didn't see it. What the hell is your game, Drummond?

Connor snorted while Roddy threw his head back and laughed. It felt good to laugh, even if danger lay just ahead of them.

Rose smiled at Gavin. She tugged on her ear and then pointed at him. *I can hear you.*

He stared at Rose as she repeated her gesture and said, "What? What is she trying to say, Roddy?"

Connor drawled, "That she's smarter than you." He glanced over his shoulder, his wry grin making Gavin visibly nervous.

Gavin spewed his next sentence out so fast that they all broke into gales of laughter. "All right. She can hear me. Why the hell didn't you say so before I made a fool of myself?"

"I thought you knew. We discussed it at Muir Castle," Connor said.

"I must not have been paying attention."

Daniel scoffed, "And that's the first time that has ever happened."

Gavin glanced at Rose sheepishly. "My apologies. No offense intended."

Rose held her hand up and shrugged. Roddy translated for her. "She says she's not upset."

The group had to settle into a single-file path, so Connor took the lead while Gavin moved into last place, making sure the lasses were safely in the middle.

————◆————

Rose leaned back against the massive chest behind her,

deciding to put her concerns behind her and enjoy the time she had with Roddy.

Her mother would be appalled by everything she'd done with Roddy—the kisses they'd shared and the way their bodies were pressing together. She'd tell her to confess her sin.

She was not sinning.

Though she knew she was an innocent, new to the ways of love, she recognized her feelings for the man behind her for what they were.

She was falling in love with Roddy Grant, just as her sire had told her she would do someday. He'd given her another piece of advice, to enjoy that feeling for as long as she could, for it could be taken away at a moment's notice. He'd stared off over the water after making that comment, causing her to question his meaning, but now she could guess. His marriage to her mother had been less than perfect.

Her sire must have finally seen her mother for the woman she was—not the kind, devout picture she presented to others. Her father must have seen the truth long ago.

She closed her eyes, letting the light banter between the cousins wash over her as she focused on the feeling of Roddy's strong thighs bracketing her hips, keeping her from jostling overmuch as the great beast moved.

She'd ridden with her sire before, but it had been nothing like this.

This was as sensual as anything she'd ever experienced, moving with her protector's comfortable rhythm. Soaking in the feel of his hand on her hip, his chest against her back, the soft rumble of his voice echoing in her ear, and his laughter ricocheting through her.

She was beginning to understand some of the things Constance had explained to her about men and women and how bairns came to be.

If she spent much more time with Roddy Grant, she'd

be so deeply in love with him that she would probably wilt like a flower when he left her after this was over. What man would wish to live a life with a woman who couldn't speak?

The cousins' talk changed tone, so she opened her eyes. They weren't far from her castle. The place that normally made her feel a wonderful sense of belonging seemed almost strange to her. As if something were on the verge of changing.

Once they arrived at a clearing a short distance from the loch, far enough away from MacDole Castle to not be seen, Rose indicated that they should stop and dismount. The smell of the sea, the songs of the birds, and the crash of the waves—all conspired to tell her they were close. The moonlight was strong, highlighting the flights of the birds and the bats.

Rose motioned to Roddy and Constance, doing her best to explain herself. Roddy translated, "The boat in the night had a beacon that could be seen from her castle." When she tried to explain the rest of her story, she moved too quickly for Roddy, but Constance understood.

Constance said, "She went down to the caves and didn't see anyone about, but she could hear the sound of lasses crying, but it sounded like it came from the dock down the shoreline."

Connor asked, "We've seen that dock, Rose. Do you know of a path near that dock? Can you lead us there without having everyone at your castle see us? Is there anywhere they could hide lasses while they waited for the boat?"

She mouthed, "Maybe, but there could be two places. I'll show you one, the other is inside the cave."

"Are you sure we won't be seen?" Gavin asked. "We're not equipped for a confrontation. We need to get information and then get word to Will."

"I can tell you it's safe," Roddy said. "'Tis where we met.

I saw her on the cliffs and followed her into caves that run underneath her home. No one else but Rose was there. She ran into the cave, and I'm guessing there's an entrance to her castle under there because she disappeared. The dock is down away from the castle."

Rose nodded.

"Lead the way, my lady," Connor said. "Show us where they might hide the lassies."

CHAPTER EIGHTEEN

R OSE GRASPED RODDY'S HAND AND started toward the shoreline, but he stopped her.

"Who's staying back?"

"Not me," Daniel said.

"Me, either," Gavin said. "I want to see the cliffs."

Connor groaned. "Fine. I'll stay back, though there's little need. This spot is well away from the regular path. In fact, once you return, Gavin can find Will and tell him this will be our meeting spot."

They all agreed and turned to follow Rose. The beginning of the path was easy to navigate, but the closer they came to the water, the steeper and more treacherous the descent. Roddy tugged on her hand, so she spun around to look at him.

"Slow down," he said. "We don't know these paths as you do, nor are we as nimble."

She smiled at the compliment, then took her time, glancing back occasionally to make sure they were keeping pace with her. When they finally reached the bottom of the rocky shore, they stood and looked out across the angry water, churning more than usual.

Gavin whistled. "I've never seen a loch churn like this."

"Our loch certainly doesn't," Roddy said.

Rose pointed above them at the swiftly moving clouds dancing in the dark of the night. *Storm coming.* Roddy shared her thoughts with the others, and it struck her that he could already read her so well.

Gavin said, "I don't know if I could even swim in that

water." He glanced at Rose and made motions to ask her if she swam in it.

She nodded, then mouthed, "Good swimmer."

Roddy gave her a look of awe and admiration. "I grew up on a loch, too, and I'm not sure I could manage those waves."

"There are no vessels in the water," Daniel said. He glanced south of their location and said, "The dock is empty. Rose, show us the caves near the castle, then we'll meet up with Will. See what he's discovered."

"This is a treacherous path," Roddy said. "I'll go with Rose. Check our meeting place to see if there's any sign of Will, then meet me in the clearing."

The group split up, promising to meet in less than an hour.

Rose scrambled up the path toward her castle from the shoreline, easily finding her way between the slippery rocks. Whenever she came to a treacherous spot, she waved her hand in warning and slowed down. Once they entered the sea cave, she held her finger to her lips. From this point on, they could possibly be heard by someone, though it was unlikely to happen on such a windy night. The two torches had stayed lit, helping them find their way.

She breathed deeply, taking in the earthy smell she was so accustomed to, as memories of her childhood excursions through the caves washed over her. Her sire used to make up tales about lassies with fins who lived in the cave.

She loved the sharp surface above their heads, made of rocks that would shine like dark diamonds when the passageway was illuminated by the fire of torches. How she wished to share her love of her land with Roddy, but this was not the time.

When they reached the door leading to the castle's cellars, she pointed for Roddy to wait, indicating that she would creep in alone.

"Absolutely not," Roddy said. "I will go with you."

Once they found their way into the passageway connected to her cellar, she stopped, holding her hand up to Roddy. She could always hear activity from this spot. From here she knew exactly who was abovestairs.

Tonight, it was hauntingly quiet.

Where was her mother?

———————◆———————

Roddy had searched the castle with Rose, and to their surprise, it was empty. She led him away from the castle and up in a different direction near the main path. When they found the main area, she veered off to the side and took him well into a copse of trees and pointed. A small hut that had probably been built by fishermen nearby sat tucked in the small forest. It could easily hold six or eight lassies. There were several stools inside, evidence that they had found the hiding spot.

Today it was empty.

Little else was there beside some shelves lined with different tools, small knives, and various types of rope. Anything they found could be used by fishermen or by the kidnappers.

"Well done, Rose," Roddy whispered as he leaned over to kiss her cheek. "They could use either spot." He motioned for her to lead the way back to the meeting place.

As soon as they found their way back, Connor came toward them on horseback. The others were fast behind him, Constance still riding with Daniel.

"What is it?" Roddy asked, recognizing the sense of urgency on his cousin's face.

"Word from Will. They think something is about to happen at the other abbey. They spotted a beacon and expect the boat to come ashore near the mouth of the firth. Not at Loch Linnhe. 'Tis less than an hour away."

"Is the other abbey that close to the firth?"

"Not as close as this one, but a good place to transport

their cargo without being seen," Daniel said.

Rose dropped her hand from Roddy's and shook her head.

Roddy peered at her, noticing her unease. She shook her head again, more emphatically. "What is it?"

Constance said, "She doesn't want to go. The guard told us about the other abbey."

"Did he have aught else to say about it?" Connor asked.

"He said the guards from Sona Abbey take many of the lasses training to be nuns there. The mean lasses, two of the ones who attacked Rose, were sent there. They were still in their punishment spot the other night, but now they've disappeared. Mayhap 'tis where they were taken."

"You mean 'tis another place used for punishment?"

"Nay, I don't think so. They're still cleaning it and preparing it for more novices. I think they were sent to work there. 'Tis a normal part of discipline—hard work so our Lord's work can be done."

Roddy had his doubts, but he didn't wish to burden her with the truth. With any luck, they would stop the worst from happening.

"She doesn't have to go," Connor said. "Neither of you do. You may stay here until we return. Gavin and Daniel, ready the horses. Roddy, you have five minutes. We won't wait any longer. Decide what you wish to do with the lasses."

Connor turned his mount around and headed off, not waiting for the others. Much like his sire, when Connor had his mind up about something, he would not be swayed.

Roddy turned to Rose. "I don't want to leave you alone."

"She won't be alone," Constance said. "I'll be here with Rose, and no one else is here to bother us." Daniel helped her down from his mount, and she waved to him as he and Gavin took off after Connor.

Rose nodded, trying to tell him something with her gestures and her mouthed words. He understood part of it.

She missed the cliffs.

"She wants to walk the cliffs," Constance said, "the place that most reminds her of her sire. I'll stay here with her. Just come back when you can."

"On one condition," Roddy said, looking Rose in the eye. "No speaking with your mother if she returns."

Rose nodded, indicating they'd stay in the chamber in the cellar near the caves if anyone returned.

Roddy arched his brow at Constance. "All right. I don't like it, but I promise to return as soon as I can." He wrapped his arms around Rose and brought her closer. Over her shoulder, he said to Constance, "Give us a minute, if you please?"

Constance blushed and spun on her heel, following the path Connor had taken to the meeting place.

Roddy couldn't stand it any longer. He cupped Rose's face and his lips locked on hers in a devouring kiss. He'd felt her soft bottom rub against him all the way from the abbey and he couldn't wait any longer.

She parted her lips and sighed, allowing his tongue to search out hers. Their tongues dueled in the dark of the night, as if none of their problems existed and the two of them were the entire world. His lips left a trail of kisses down her neck and to her ear, whispering sweet words as they did so, and her response was to tip her head back to give him better access to her neck, her hands sliding up to grip his tunic. He cupped her breasts through her mantle, frustrated that he couldn't feel her skin, but she arched against him nonetheless, telling him she was as eager for him as he was for her.

"Roddy!"

Daniel rode up behind him, leading his horse by the reins, so he ended the kiss and said, "I promise I'll be back as soon as I can."

He kissed her lightly on the lips and waited with her until Constance returned. The only words he could think of were, "Be careful."

He mounted his horse and tugged on the reins. Unable to stop himself, he glanced back once and had to smile. Constance was pulling Rose toward the castle while Rose stared back at him. She lifted her hand in a brief wave before turning around.

Daniel snorted. "Are you going to thank me?"

Roddy pulled his horse abreast of Daniel's and said, "For what? I wish you'd taken longer."

Daniel drawled, "If I hadn't come along, you'd have bedded her, and I'd be taking you both to the abbey to get married."

Roddy shook his head, annoyed by the implication. "You're such an arse sometimes, Ghost. After all my mother endured, I would never treat a lass that way." Before meeting his sire, his mother had been abused by a bad man. His sire had told him the story when he was old enough to understand it.

Daniel arched a brow at Roddy, then sent his horse into a full gallop. Roddy did the same, and easily matched his pace.

They hadn't traveled far when an odd feeling overtook Roddy. He glanced up at the sky, noticing a few birds circling overhead—the falcons and one other. He couldn't shake the strange sensation, but he couldn't decide exactly what to do about it either.

Not long after, they caught sight of a few horses up ahead. Braden and Will had dismounted and were talking with Maggie, Gregor, and Uncle Brodie.

Once they came alongside of them and dismounted, Roddy asked, "Your headache is gone, Maggie?"

She gave him a look that told him the reason she was here was not a good one. Sighing, she whispered, "Aye, my headache is better but only because I know what's to come." She beckoned them all closer so they could talk quietly. Even though no one else was around, he guessed talking loudly would risk bringing Maggie's headache back. "I fell asleep and dreamed of two people working together against one. One was of the cloth—man or woman, I couldn't be sure. The other was verra wealthy, and I'm quite sure 'twas a woman. They were discussing two large shipments of lasses. Some were in nuns' clothing. And I saw one other strange thing. A bird."

"Was it one of my falcons, do you think?" Will asked. The falcons called out overhead as if they knew they were the topic of discussion.

Roddy glanced up at them—and when one of them swooped down, he realized he recognized the third bird of prey circling them.

Braden echoed his thoughts, "'Tis an owl."

"Hellfire, nay." Roddy's gut clenched in response to the soft "hoo" the bird called down to him. He knew at once it was the same owl he'd seen at the abbey.

"What does he want?" Braden muttered, stepping away from the group.

"I know not," Roddy said. "But I'm going to find out if I can."

"Shite, Roddy! Is that the same one you saw before?" Daniel asked, as they all stared up into the sky.

Roddy rubbed the rough stubble of his beard. "I think so, but I won't know until I see it up close. I need to see its eyes."

"We'll get him down here then," Will said, his confidence obvious as he strode over to his horse. "You know I would trust any warning or foreboding from a bird."

The creature swooped in closer, hooting several times as if to get someone's attention.

Will pulled something from his horse's saddle and carried it over to Roddy. "Here," he said, setting the bit of fabric on his arm, "See if he'll alight." He arranged it carefully and stepped back. "Hold your arm up."

"What the hell does an owl have to do with all this?"

Gavin asked, seemingly mystified.

Uncle Brodie said, "You don't question certain things, lad. You just accept them, whatever the reason. Step out farther, Roddy. He fears the rest of us."

"Agreed," Will said. "Move away and lift your arm higher. I'll send my falcons off." He waved his arms and the two creatures flew away. The owl dipped even closer. "And when he lands, the rest of you are to be quiet. This is between the owl and Roddy." He motioned them all back a few steps.

The owl looked as though it had tall, erect ears, though Roddy knew them to be just feathers. He stared at it in wonder as it swooped even farther down, almost alighting on his arm, but then glided up again, as if checking to see all was safe.

"Don't move, Roddy."

The bird began to make snapping sounds intermittent with squeals, odd sounds he'd never heard a bird make before.

"He's not going to attack him, will he, Will?" Maggie asked.

"Nay. Hold strong, Roddy. He'll fly straight at you, then lift his wings vertically to slow his descent. His talons will come at you first."

Roddy held still with his arm extended, stunned as he watched the large owl come at him just as Will had described. He fought the urge to run from the bird of prey's talons and held solid until the big bird landed on the material Will had provided to protect his skin.

"'Tis the same one, Roddy?" Daniel asked, but Will shushed him.

Roddy stared at the great bird, its wings now tucked in at its sides, its goldish orange eyes fixed on Roddy's. "Greetings, my friend."

The owl snapped its beak several times again, its wings lifting briefly before it tucked them in again. It couldn't speak to him in the traditional manner, but he could intuit its message much as he could intuit the meaning of Rose's gestures and mouthed words.

"Rose is in trouble, isn't she?" he asked. "You want me to go after her, do you not?"

The owl closed his eyes as if in relief and said "hoo" three times.

CHAPTER NINETEEN

R OSE LED CONSTANCE TO SOME of her favorite spots on the cliffs, demonstrating her agility on the rocks. Her friend had a more difficult time clambering over the rocks, though mayhap that was not so surprising. The gowns given to them by the abbey weren't exactly conducive to free movement. They were moving across one more set of rocks down near the edge of the loch when Rose saw something from the corner of her eye. She held her hand up to her friend. They both came to a stop, and Rose pointed out toward the loch.

Then she saw it again.

A beacon.

Constance gasped. "I saw that." Her voice dropped to the barest of whispers. "Is that what they're looking for, Rose?"

Rose traced the letters of the word "bad" on Constance's palm.

"Och, if 'tis bad, we must leave. We can go after Roddy." A worried look rose on her face. "Nay, we don't have horses, do we?" Her finger played with her lower lip. "What shall we do? We had best hide. I don't wish to see your mother. Though it doesn't mean she'll be here, does it? How many servants work for her?"

Rose held up three fingers, then gripped her friend's hand and led her back to the caves. They could sneak inside the castle and stay in the cellars. There they would be able to hear anything that took place in the castle or in the caves.

They found their way into the cellars of the castle, and

Rose led Constance into a small chamber with two beds in it. "What shall we do?" Constance asked. "There's a ship coming this way. Is it docking here or at the other place? Why would it shine a beacon? Who could it be signaling? There's no one here. I don't understand. Oh, where are the lads? We need them."

Constance tended to babble when she was upset, so Rose let her do so. Then she heard the voice she'd dreaded.

Her mother.

She was arguing with someone, but Rose couldn't hear the other voice.

"Why did you allow the child to leave? If I'm lucky, the fool will get lost in the forest and eaten by a pack of wolves. She's always been naught but trouble to me, ever since the day she was born."

Constance jerked and grabbed both of her hands. "Rose, I'm so sorry," she whispered.

Rose shook her head, attempting to tell her friend not to be sorry for her. She knew her mother was a cruel woman…and yet, the words had a bite. Her own mother wished her dead.

"And I hope you're not going to turn out to be the fool Walter was. He coddled that lass as if he'd given birth to her himself."

"Now, Jean. Forget about your daughter for the moment. We must deal with this exchange. The other one failed, so this one must go ahead if you wish to make coin. Your friend in England may not send us another ship if we don't make this shipment. We can deal with Rose when she turns up, and she will. For now, you must follow my lead. You've never dealt with these men before, and trust me, they are not what you'd call an ethical lot."

Rose and Constance stared at each other, wide-eyed. Did Constance recognize the voice the same way she had?

"Father Seward," Constance whispered. "I'm frightened, Rose."

Her mother's usual vindictive tone bounced off the stone walls of the castle. "Your abbey has sloppy guardsmen. How could they not notice a lass sneaking out of an abbey? For heaven's sake, there were two lasses."

"I told you, they were stolen away by several young warriors. My guards tried to follow them, but two of the men lost their lives because of it. I was not willing to lose any more of them until this exchange is made. There are seven lasses."

"Find my daughter and her friend and we'll sell them, also."

Constance gasped and gripped Rose's arm, the fear in her eyes clear, but Rose would not allow her mother to control her any longer. She would not let her win, not when the stakes were so high.

She patted Constance's hand and mouthed the words, "Do not worry. The lads will come." This seemed to calm her friend a bit, but she was still noticeably upset. Would she be able to stay calm when the time came to act?

Rose checked the dagger sewn inside her gown. *She* would stay calm, without a doubt.

Her mother began to pace, the sound of her footfalls echoing through the drafty old castle. "Where would those lads take my daughter and her friend?"

"They're not here, my sweet. Stop worrying your pretty head about it. In fact, we have just enough time for a brief tumble in your sheets before the boat arrives. No one else is here except your steward, and he's busy down by the dock."

"Nay. We have to find her. I want her on the boat," her mother said with a surprising amount of vehemence.

Father Seward said, "Nay, we've agreed. She's not going on the boat. I want her to stay."

"I know, Bernard. I know you're fond of the lass and wish to keep her at the new abbey, but I've changed my mind. I'll get good coin for her. She's suspicious and I don't like it. I want her gone. What if she remembers?"

Father Seward's pleasant tone changed in an instant, his voice loud enough to cover Constance's shocked gasp. "I don't care if you don't like it. We had an agreement and you'll stick to it."

The two lasses stared at each other in disbelief.

"Bernard, are you suggesting what I think you are? She's much too young for you."

"You said you wish to go back to England. You'll never have to see her again once you leave. She'll live at Abbey of Angels. I'll tell her you died, if you like. But I'll not give her up."

Roddy pushed his horse to the point of exhaustion, driven by the fear of something happening to Rose. He couldn't stomach the thought of anything happening to her, hadn't realized how much she meant to him. He'd quite liked having her tucked in front of him on his horse and holding her in his arms to kiss her senseless.

Why didn't it bother him that she couldn't speak?

Because it didn't. Others would probably question him, mayhap even call him a fool, but she was a quick learner, and soon she'd be fluent in reading and writing. They could communicate that way.

Daniel and Connor were at his side, and another friend, the owl, flew just ahead of him as if leading the way.

Will yelled to them from behind. They'd just crested the highest spot along the loch, giving them a panoramic view of the water. Roddy tried to understand him, but he couldn't until he noticed Will's pointing finger.

The beacon had passed the spot where they'd thought it would dock at the firth, instead heading straight for Mac-Dole Castle.

The owl's cry filled the air.

Roddy refused to let his fear get to him.

The owl would lead them straight back to Rose.

———◆———

Rose cracked open the door to their chamber in the cellars because she could no longer hear clearly. Her mother's voice had dropped, and she'd missed something she'd said, but Father Seward answered her clearly enough to be heard down on the loch.

"Jean, you are a cruel woman. I cannot believe anyone would treat their own child the way you've treated that sweet lass. For heaven's sake, she can't hear or speak."

"Oh, you dimwitted hedgehog. I've told you she can hear quite well. I just frightened her enough never to speak again. You helped me scare her or do you not recall? You tied her down and held her."

"But she was so medicated she does not remember. Does that memory not haunt you? I'll hear that child's screams for the rest of my life."

Her mother began to mutter and pace again, but Rose could barely hear it. A sick feeling had begun to creep from her core through her limbs. Something caught in her mind, something Father Seward had said. How he'd held her down. Why? What had happened to her? She had to know. Her mother would not get away with any more secrets.

It sounded as if her mother had dropped something heavy, but the sound felt far away. "Rose," Constance said, shaking her arm. She'd obviously said it a few times already. "Rose? What did she do to you? Oh, you poor thing. How have you survived to be the sweet lass you are with such a cruel mother?"

Suddenly the lies and secrets all weighed a little too much. Without thinking on it, Rose pushed the door open and chased up the stairway in a fury.

What had her mother done to her?

CHAPTER TWENTY

———◆———

ROSE OPENED THE DOOR AT the top of the stairs, made haste through the kitchens and into the great hall, where she was surprised to find her mother alone.

Her mother leapt up from her seat at one of the trestle tables. She greeted her quite appropriately, or so Rose thought.

"You daft bitch. Where have you been? I've been looking everywhere for you. Have you not caused me enough trouble?" She raced over to Rose and grabbed her by the arm, squeezing her hard enough to bruise the skin. She pulled her other arm back to deliver a slap.

Rose didn't give her the chance, instead taking advantage of her balance to shove the woman, something that clearly shocked Lady MacDole because she fell against the table, hitting her head hard.

Constance came up beside her, her eyes fearful but determined, and said to her mother, "You are a cruel bitch, are you not? Who treats their own daughter the way you have?"

Her mother pushed herself away from the table and came at Constance, reaching out to slap her friend, but Rose was faster, catching her arm and pushing her backward. That wasn't enough to stop her frenzied mother. She charged around the table for Constance, grabbing her by the hair and yanking her backward. "Rose, you'll do as I say or I'll hurt her."

No longer afraid of the woman, Rose corralled the fury inside her into something strong. She mouthed the words,

"Let. Her. Go."

Her mother laughed. "I'll do as I wish with her. In fact, there's a ship on its way here. If you don't do as I ask, I'll sell her to the men on that ship. They'll pay me good coin for her. Unless you wish to lose your friend, you'll heed my words." She dragged Constance over to the wall, yanking a dagger down from a display case carrying weaponry. This she held at Constance's back.

Rose stared at her friend, who had begun to tremble, doing her best to tell her to be strong.

"Go down the staircase, Rose," her mother said. "We'll be directly behind you. Do not run away or I'll stab your friend in the back. Do as I say and I won't hurt her."

Rose knew exactly what her mother intended. She was going to lock them into the chamber in the cellar.

She couldn't allow that to happen. She had to stop her before they reached the staircase. Rose slowed her steps just to annoy her mother. How she hated it when her daughter didn't do exactly as she was instructed. Then Rose's eyes fell on exactly what she needed.

"Stop delaying the inevitable, Rose," her mother snapped. "Go down the staircase and hurry."

To throw her mother off a wee bit more, she began to walk in a strange path, teetering one way and then the other.

"Rose MacDole. Do as I say!"

Rose continued meandering, swinging her arms out as if she needed the help to stay balanced.

"Rose, I'm warning you!"

She swung her arms one way and then the other, back and forth, giving herself a wide berth. At the last second, she grabbed two apples from a crate on a table and flung them at her mother, one catching her in the forehead, the shock of the blow forcing her to drop the dagger. Constance squealed and ran free.

Using one of the moves Roddy had taught her, Rose

grabbed her mother, spun her around, and pinned her to the floor among the rushes. Yanking out her dagger, she held it against her mother's throat.

Her mother spewed hatred. "For once, you've surprised me. I did not know you had the strength to do such a thing. You've always been so weak."

Rose couldn't handle the vile words coming from her mother's mouth. She mouthed the words she wished to tell her, starting with, "Hate you. Cruel." Then she looked at Constance for assistance, mouthing a few words to her because she knew her friend would get her point across better than she ever could.

"I'd be glad to tell her for you. How could you be so mean? You told her having her courses was punishment for kissing a lad. How could you say such a thing? You intended for her to stay at the abbey forever, didn't you? She'd never stop having her courses so she'd never return here, would she? Just because you loved Father Seward? What else do you wish for me to tell her, Rose?"

Constance began to pace through the hall while Rose considered what else she wished to say to her mother, but her friend's gasp stopped her.

"Oh, Rose. Nay…"

Rose glanced at her friend, not understanding the reason she sounded so upset. Constance stared in horror at something on the floor in the corner, hidden behind several tables. How she wished she could scream at her friend to tell her what she was looking at, but she could not. As ever, the words were stuck in her throat. She was so discomfited by Constance that her grip loosened a touch on the dagger at her mother's throat, allowing the odious woman to speak.

Her mother said the most chilling words she'd ever heard.

"Your friend is looking at Father Seward. I killed him."

Rose jerked her gaze back to her mother.

"I did the same to your father."

The expression on her mother's face made her want to heave, but worse, her vision began to dim. Her own mother had killed her dear sire, and now she'd killed again. She lifted her gaze to Constance again, surprised to see her run toward the door, her gaze full of fear.

All she could think was, "Run, Constance."

Once the door opened and her friend disappeared, a searing pain erupted in her head.

The world went black.

Roddy was the first to arrive, just as a bolt of lightning ripped across the sky above, bright enough to light up the area. The view reminded him of the night he and Connor had seen the ghost, making him wonder what more could possibly happen. A harrowing scream rent the air as the clouds above them erupted in a downpour. The scream came from a lass running haphazardly down the path, unsure of which way she should go, unaccustomed to the rough terrain. They were still a distance from the castle, so he was surprised she'd made it this far.

Constance.

His heart felt like it would explode out of his chest.

Daniel and Roddy dismounted and raced toward her, Daniel scooping her up and holding her tightly to him so she wouldn't run away.

"Constance, calm down. What's wrong?" Daniel yelled, but the poor lass continued to scream, her fists clenched tight as if she wished to punch something.

Or someone.

Roddy noticed the small hut Rose had shown him wasn't far, so he pointed to it because it would provide them with cover against the pelting rain.

As soon as they were inside, Roddy reached for Constance's hand and said, "Constance, where is Rose?"

She stared at him, the fear in her face so obvious that it

tore into his already agitated heart. What the hell had happened to Rose? Were they too late?

Will, Maggie, and the rest joined them inside the small hut, just barely able to hold them all. Constance continued to shake her head, mumbling incoherently.

Daniel sat on a stool in the corner and settled Constance on his lap. Then he gently cupped her face with his one hand, turning her gaze toward him. "Constance, look at me. 'Tis Daniel. Remember me? I helped you and Rose at the abbey. Roddy and I are here to help you both. We've brought friends with us. Do you remember me?"

Constance's gaze locked on his and she nodded, gulping.

"Good. Rose. Where is Rose?" His tone was so gentle, unlike anything Roddy had ever heard from the boisterous lad with the sharp sense of humor.

After several swallows, Constance finally explained, "Rose's mother. She killed Father Seward." She gripped Daniel's upper arm. "I saw him. I walked away from Rose and I went past some tables and there he was on the floor. Blood was pooling around him and a knife lay nearby. They had been talking about a beacon in the loch and an exchange. But we overheard them, and Rose wanted to confront her mother. She held her at knifepoint. Rose's mother…she admitted to killing Rose's father long ago, and Rose lost her focus. Some man came up behind her and hit her over the head, and I ran, and I don't know where they took her and…Roddy, please save Rose."

He was already pacing back and forth in the small space they had, ready to break into a run. Desperate to get to her.

"How long ago, lass?" Will asked.

"A while ago. Mayhap a quarter of an hour or half an hour?"

Maggie took over. "Roddy, can you lead us to the caves and the dock?"

Roddy nodded.

"Who's the strongest swimmer?" Will asked.

Gavin, Daniel, Connor, and Braden all pointed to Roddy.

Maggie issued her instructions. "Constance will show me where she found Father Seward. We'll check for Rose inside. If we don't find her, we'll join you once she's feeling calmer. Connor, Braden, and Roddy, down to the docks. Will and Gavin, get to higher ground with your bows. Uncle Brodie, would you and Daniel act as our lookouts in the cave?" When he nodded, she continued, "Did anyone see a boat we could use if we need to reach that galley ship?"

Daniel said, "I saw one rowboat near the dock."

"Keep that in mind. Constance, we suspect they're exchanging lasses. Did you hear any more about their plan? Mayhap how many lasses they have?"

She nodded, trembling. "Seven. Her mother wanted Rose and me on that boat, too." With her hand on her throat, she declared, "She wanted to sell her own daughter."

Rose awakened with an awful headache, her hands and feet tied together, something that felt achingly familiar. Male voices echoed around her, but she ignored them, instead trying to figure out where they'd taken her.

It didn't take long for the rolling and crashing of the waves to let her know she was on some type of boat. She lifted her head briefly to look about her, only to drop it back onto the rough surface beneath her as a wave of pain pounded through it. Unfortunately, she'd been able to determine one thing when she lifted her head.

The boat was a large one with many rowers, and they were far from shore.

"One of them has awakened," a voice shouted. "What shall I do with her?"

Another answered, "Naught. 'Tis the one who cannot speak. Do not concern yourself."

Her gaze traveled the area around her. Several other lasses were tied up and asleep. She thought she recognized Ada and another girl who ate quietly by herself, but it was difficult for her to focus between the rolling of the ship, her headache, and the streaks of lightning overhead. A storm pounded down on the ship, all lightning and thunder and sheeting rain. The wind caught in the sails, shaking the ship. The boat was what her sire had called a birlinn, and they were tucked in a cargo space with a tarp intended to protect them from the rain, but she was still drenched and shivering.

She lifted her head again, doing her best not to jolt it, sighing with relief because at least Constance was not on the boat.

Mayhap she'd gotten away. How she prayed it was so. The last thing she recalled was seeing her friend run toward the door as pain radiated through her head.

The dagger she'd held to her mother's throat was almost certainly gone. Despite being tied up, she managed to check her other hidden dagger she'd tucked into her boot. To her relief, the second dagger hadn't been taken from her. She had a chance.

Her mother. She'd wished to kill the evil woman who'd slain her father, but she hadn't. Several tears trailed down the side of her face and landed on the hull of the ship, but she couldn't allow her emotions to overtake her. She needed to stay strong for Roddy and Constance.

And for herself.

Her mother, the evil witch, had been carrying on with Father Seward. The man who'd been so kind to her was a bad man. He'd wanted her more than he'd wanted her mother, and that was what had angered Lady MacDole enough to kill him. But they'd said something about the past…

Something dark and horrible niggled at the back of her brain. Something too awful to comprehend.

Her tongue felt swollen and wrong in her mouth, and she found herself thinking of what Roddy had asked her about the tip of her tongue.

Someone had cut it off.

In an instant, she was back on the table years ago, struggling with the ties at her feet and her hands, trying to kick the two men who'd tied her down, two men who had been with her family for years. She'd screamed and cried and kicked. Father Seward had remembered that scream.

She'd had a voice.

Her mother had shouted to be heard above Rose's keening. "Hold her down, I said. How much can a wee lass hurt you?"

She saw the knife come at her, the hands holding her head fast on either side.

And then she remembered everything.

She was outside in a storm that night, too. She and her father were out on the cliffs when the storm unleashed a deluge. They stood there together, watching the lightning, but after a brief spell, he insisted that she return to the castle.

She agreed because she wasn't overly fond of storms. Rather than head home through the front gate, she took the other path, the one through the cellars. Just before she entered the caves, she heard her mother's voice.

When she looked back, she saw her mother standing opposite her father, screaming at him. She pushed him and he nearly lost his balance, but instead of shouting at the woman, he did the honorable thing and turned away, heading down the path toward the caves. He didn't even say a word in the face of all of that violent rage.

Rose closed her eyes because she hated to see her parents fighting. When she finally opened them, it was too late to call out and warn her sire. Her mother gave him a huge shove from behind, forcing him over the edge of the cliffs to a certain death below.

An endless scream erupted from Rose. Her dear sire was dead. She'd watched her own mother commit murder. She screamed and screamed and could hardly recall what happened afterward until she noticed another man headed straight for her—their steward.

Her mother was furious with her.

In a state of shock, she didn't even attempt to fight the steward when he lifted her up and carried her into the great hall, pinning her to the table while her mother barked instructions at everyone. She fought her bindings, but she lost the battle, blood dripping down her arm because her skin was raw from the rope.

Her mother came at her in a fury, yelling at the man behind her. "Hold her head."

Then she reached in, grabbed Rose's tongue with some odd tool and used a knife to cut the tip of it off.

Rose screamed and screamed in pain, both physical and emotional.

Her mother left her tied to the table for the entire night, the flashing of the lightning paralyzing her in fear.

The next morning her mother came down and showed her the tip of her tongue, all bloody, and said, "Now, if you ever mention a word of what you saw, I'll cut your entire tongue out and you'll never be able to speak again. I'll send you to an island and leave you there. You are the devil, I swear it."

She didn't remember much after that. She'd gone inside herself, not speaking to anyone because they'd all turned against her. Her mother's steward, Harold, had been a part of the cruelty. Another man had been present, too—one whose voice she now recognized as that of Father Seward.

At twelve winters, she hadn't guessed the truth. Her sire had discovered her mother with another man, and she'd killed him rather than face the consequences.

The incident had been too much for her to handle.

She became the perfect child, never speaking, never

making any noise, and spending most of her time outside. Until now, the memory of that day had stayed deeply buried, the horror hidden from her conscious mind.

It was time for that charade to end. She would never again let her mother lead her about, never again believe everything the twisted woman told her.

Rose edged the knife out of its hiding place and sliced her bonds. Then she pounded at the tarp until it gave way, giving her the ability to push herself to a sitting position. Fortunately, the crew ignored her. The men fought hard to control the sails and the driving wind, oblivious to their cargo. She made her way over to the edge of the boat and opened her mouth, but nothing came out.

She hadn't lost the ability to speak at all. She'd buried it deep inside in order to survive, but that time was behind her. She would be strong for Roddy, for her sire, and most importantly, for herself.

Tears filled her eyes, but she swallowed them down, pushing herself. She tried again, opening her mouth, trying as hard as she could to make any sound at all, but to no avail. Thinking to start small, she attempted a hum, but she failed to get beyond the small whirr she'd always been able to expel.

She leaned toward the edge of the boat, reaching for the power to project her voice.

Someone finally saw her, for she heard a man's voice shout, "Get her. Sit on her, tie her down. Do something!"

Two men charged straight for her, but an owl swooped down in the billowing wind and flew in front of her. Just as one bastard reached out to grab her, the owl struck the scum's hands with its powerful talons.

Her new friend. The owl had to be the same one she'd met at the abbey, and her sire had sent it to assist her.

She would do this for him, too.

She closed her eyes, pulled from her belly and opened her mouth. To her delight, the loudest scream she'd ever heard tore loose from her own vocal cords.

"Roddy!" She was so elated with her accomplishment that she laughed and cried at the same time because it was her own melodic voice she heard.

"Roddy, Roddy! Help me!"

Rose could indeed talk.

CHAPTER TWENTY-ONE

RODDY, CONNOR, AND BRADEN ALL headed toward the dock on foot, having left their horses above the cliff path. To his surprise, the owl headed out over the water, leaving them. As they neared the edge of the loch, an eerie feeling unfurled in Roddy's belly. His fear of dying had returned.

The fear that he could not do what he needed to do to save Rose's life nearly unmanned him, but he wouldn't let it stop him.

He would save Rose. He loved her.

Truer words he'd never thought. He was in love with Rose MacDole, and that love was strong enough to overcome any kind of fear. He'd do whatever it took to keep her from being sent away in that boat.

The storm pelted on, waves crashing so hard it was difficult for them to hear one another. Roddy lowered his hand to the hilt of his sword as he reached the dock. "There's no boat. It isn't here yet," he roared, shouting to be heard above the din of the storm.

Connor and Braden came up behind him, their gazes searching the rough waters and the shoreline for any sign of a boat or people.

Naught.

Connor shouted and pointed out into the middle of the loch. "There. A birlinn."

"Good," Braden said. "We're here in time. We'll catch them when they land and put an end to this. But where are the men on shore?"

"Shite!" Roddy yelled, dropping his sword on the ground. He began yanking off his plaid and tunic, not stopping until he stood only in his trews.

"What the hell, Roddy?" Connor asked, stupefied. "What are you doing?"

"The boat's going *away* from us. It's too far away."

He tugged one boot off as Braden said, "You can't go after it. With that sail up, it's moving much faster than you can swim. Besides, the waves are so large they'll overtake you. We need to find that rowboat."

Roddy removed his other boot and argued with his cousin. "Then go find a boat and come after me. I'm going in."

"Think on this, Roddy," Connor said. "The lightning could kill you in an instant. And you don't know if Rose is even on it. She could be inside the castle."

He paused, considering the possibility that Connor was right, but a voice came to him just then, very faint but clear as a bell.

"Roddy!"

Without a doubt, he was certain he knew that voice. "That's Rose," he said in wonder. "I'm going in. Find help to come after us. I can't bring all the lasses back."

"You're not thinking clearly," Connor said, grabbing his arm, "Rose can't talk, remember?"

As if to disagree with Connor's statement, the voice called out to him again. "Roddy, Roddy, help me!"

"That's Rose. I'd know her voice anywhere." He'd never felt so sure of anything in his life. His soul recognized her, but how did one explain that?

Braden said, "Godspeed. We'll go for help, but you already have some."

Roddy dove into the water, not waiting for Braden to finish his comment, but it came to him a second later as it carried across the water. "The owl, Roddy. He flew over here from the area near the ship and now he's heading back to the ship. We'll get the boat."

He closed his mouth and concentrated on his strokes, pulling from his gut to stay focused.

Rose needed him.

And his sweet Rose could speak.

———◆———

Rose assured herself she was as strong as they came. She'd endured torture, brainwashing, and more. She would find a way off this boat.

The owl had flown away, as if summoned by something, but she'd managed to stop the two attackers. She kicked one in the groin as Roddy had shown her and struck the other in his groin with her fist. Another came at her, so she grabbed the dagger she'd used to cut her bonds and sliced across his leg, causing blood to soak his trews. The brute stepped away from her, bellowing.

A voice called to her from the inky depths of the firth. "Rose? I'm coming."

Roddy. Oh, how she loved him.

She couldn't wait to use her newfound voice to tell him so.

Two more men came at her, and to her delight, the owl swooped back into sight. It struck the man with one of its talons while a falcon landed on the other's head and pecked him. The big oaf squealed like a laddie.

"What the hell is with these birds?" someone shouted in a voice edged with fear. Another bird swooped down, slicing into someone's arm. The bird came at him again, frightening him so badly he jumped over the side of the boat. Men were pulled from their rowing to fight the creatures attacking them from above. Two falcons and the dear owl didn't let up but continued to dive at the men, scaring a few more overboard. The owl landed on the rigging of the sail and tried to tug it loose, but it wouldn't come free. Rose reached over with her dagger and cut the rope, collapsing one side of the sail to slow its course.

The man who'd been standing at the head of the boat yelled, "You foolish bitch. I don't care how much I'd get for you. You're going overboard."

Three men lunged at her. She kicked and screamed, fighting them off, but one man got her in a chokehold. She bit him, breaking free, and one of his companions croaked, "Can you not control a wee bitch? Is she too tough for you?"

A large wave hit them, catapulting two of them over the side, saving her and giving her enough leeway to lurch toward the front of the boat. Clinging to the side, she stepped over the young lasses who were still restrained and asleep. When she reached the end, she realized Euphemie was the last girl in the row.

She had awakened and sat up with a shocked expression on her face. The gag in her mouth prevented her from speaking, but she motioned for Rose to remove it.

She debated the merits of doing something nice for the lass who'd been so cruel, but no one deserved to be sold like an object. Not even Euphemie. Rose tugged on the cloth and tossed it over the side, then continued on her way.

"Rose!" Euphemie called to her.

Rose grabbed the side of the boat to steady herself and turned around to face the other girl.

"You can hear and talk," the girl said, stating the obvious. Then she paused and said, "Why are you being kind to me?"

Rose realized that it was time for her to start speaking to everyone. "Because I'm not like you at all." She turned her back and continued on to the edge of the boat.

"I'm sorry, Rose," Euphemie hollered. "I was wrong about you."

Rose ignored her, unsure of whether or not to believe her, but it didn't matter. She had to find a way to safety and that was her focus.

She reached the end of the boat and could go no farther. Staring into the depths of the water, she briefly thought about jumping over, but the man she thought was the captain grabbed her from behind and wrapped his hands around her throat in a choke-hold. Gasping for air, she scratched and kicked, but she was losing the battle. Her vision dimmed as he increased his pressure on her windpipe.

To her surprise, a giant shape loomed over the side of the boat and lunged directly at the captain, knocking him off his feet.

Roddy Grant had arrived.

He fought like a man possessed, his fists striking anyone near him and making quick work of the few remaining men. Then he turned to Rose, a smile on his face.

Had she ever seen anything so wonderful in her life?

Another wave caught them and sent her flying into his arms. He clutched her to him and whispered, "You can talk."

And so she told him the most important thought in her mind, just in case her ability to speak suddenly disappeared.

She smiled and said, "I love you, Roddy Grant."

CHAPTER TWENTY-TWO

———◆———

RODDY HELPED ROSE INTO THE boat Braden and Connor had located and rowed over. The rain had slowed to a light drizzle by then.

"Daniel and Uncle Brodie found a larger boat in the caves," Connor said. "They're on their way to assist with the others. Will said he'd find a third boat."

"Good. I dropped the anchor and dumped the few dead bodies over the side. A few of the villains are trying their best to swim to shore, but they were headed away from us. Most of the lasses are still asleep from some concoction they were given. A couple of men are still alive, but we tied them up, hoping Maggie and Will would be able to glean some information from them."

Braden glanced at the rocking galley ship. There was no movement inside. "Good, because I don't think we can hold more than you two. I don't want to weigh this small boat down any more. I'll not risk capsizing it in these waves. We'll take you back, then bring a larger crew to row this one back to shore."

Roddy sat in the middle and wrapped his arms around Rose, settling her on his lap.

As they shoved back toward shore, Connor and Braden rowing, Connor said, "I wanted to bring a dry plaid, but couldn't locate one."

Peering up into Roddy's gaze, Rose said, "I'm warm enough."

"Lass, you found your voice," Braden said. "We heard it carry across the water. Well done. Never seen Roddy act without thinking like that."

Connor said, "Aye, you lost all those fears in a hurry, did you not, cousin? You dove into a sea loch rolling from the storm, not giving a care about being struck by lightning."

Roddy glanced over the waves they battled to get back to shore, just then noticing the size of the crests and the way the water continued to batter their small boat. He glanced at Braden in front of him. "The water was a wee bit rough, but 'twas not that bad." The fear of dying had descended on him as they found their way down the treacherous path to the shoreline, but it had left him and never returned.

Braden muttered, "Never seen my sire pace so much. Said your sire would kill him for allowing you in that water."

Roddy couldn't help but chuckle, for he knew nothing would have stopped him. "He wouldn't have been able to convince me to wait. I was driven by the sound of a wee voice across the water."

"Wee voice?" Connor said, clucking his tongue. "That was a strong voice, not a wee one."

Once they were close to shore, another voice carried to them. "Rose? Are you hale? Rose. Tell me 'tis true you can speak." Constance stood at the edge of the rocks, watching for them. Her body nearly shook with sobs.

"Constance, I feel the best I ever have. Cease your worry," Rose shouted, a rippling wave of applause following her declaration.

When they reached shore, Daniel and Will came over to assist them, but they were shoved aside by Rose's dear friend, who reached for her as soon as Roddy lifted her over the side. Constance grabbed her in a bear hug and cried all over her shoulder. "I'm glad 'twas raining so you're already wet." She paused to swipe at her tears. "Say something else. Please?"

Rose said, "You are the best friend I could ever have asked for."

"Oh, Rose," Constance squealed and hugged her friend again. "You're soaked. We can go dry off in the hut. Maggie went inside your castle and found some dry clothes for both of us."

Constance led her up the path to the hut at the top of the cliffs, people gathered all around it.

Roddy couldn't be any prouder of his cousins and how they'd pulled together to accomplish something so important.

"How many, Roddy?"

"That's eight more you've saved, Maggie."

"*We've* saved."

A harsh voice carried over to them. "There she is. There's my dear daughter. She'll tell you how I had naught to do with this. She cannot speak, but she can hear. Just ask her questions and she'll tell you." She held her bound hands up for all to see. "She was there. She's a witness. Untie me so I can hug my sweet girl. Father Seward tried to kill me. Kill me! 'Twas self-defense."

Roddy spun around and stared at her wretched mother. How he wished to pick the woman up and throw her down the path, letting her bounce her way down across the gravel, but this was Rose's chance to finally speak with her mother. He would not take it away from her. "We meet again. Rose, if I were you, I'd ignore her and walk away. She's not worth your effort."

Rose gripped his hand tightly, fury crossing her face. "Oh, but you're wrong about that. She *is* worth my effort."

———◆———

Rose had been so happy to see Roddy that she hadn't given a thought to what she would do when she saw her mother again. Numerous ideas bounced around in her mind, but one in particular seemed to win her over.

She strolled over to her mother as silence descended over the group. "Nay, Mama. You did kill Father Seward, and you also killed my dear father. You frightened me so much at the age of twelve that I didn't speak for five years. No longer. I now know you for who you are." Rose turned toward Maggie and Will. "This woman pushed my sire off a cliff five years ago, and she just killed Father Seward. She belongs in prison."

Her mother's only response was to start laughing. The sound of the woman's laughter grated on Rose's nerves—a wicked sound, one she wished she could slap out of her—but she didn't wish to dirty her hands on the woman. Lady MacDole was so vile and devious that she would no longer allow her to have any power over her. Even the power of hate.

Rose shook her head. "You are not worth my effort. I want naught to do with you." Roddy's hand settled on the small of her back, and his other hand squeezed her hip in support.

Her mother's head tipped back with another wild cackle, only this time, the laughter came to an abrupt halt. She screamed, bringing her face back up in a flash, an expression of sheer horror on her face. She spat and spat and squealed, finally shouting, "Harold, kill that foul bird! Look what he did to me."

She stared up to the sky just as a long-eared owl swooped down and landed another dropping on one side of her mother's face.

The entire group erupted into laughter as the owl swooped down at the foul woman again, causing her to duck and swing reflexively at the bird. "Harold, Harold. Stop this beast. Daughter, you better put a stop to this or I'll…I'll…"

Rose strode over and stuffed a filthy piece of tarp into her mother's mouth. "Close *your* mouth, or I'll cut *your* tongue out."

Then she strode over to the entrance to her castle.

She never looked back.

———◆———

Roddy followed Rose into her castle, but to his surprise, she led him through the cellars and out onto the cliffs. They stood there overlooking the water, which he'd quickly realized was her favorite place.

He came up behind her and wrapped his arms around her, whispering in her ear, "What are you thinking, my love?"

She turned and wrapped her arms around his neck, stepping up on her tiptoes to give him a quick kiss on the lips. Pulling back slightly, she said, "I'm thinking how much I love you, Roddy Grant. Thank you for believing in me and supporting me through all of this." Tears misted in her eyes.

"If you love me half as much as I love you, then mayhap you'll consider marrying me," he whispered.

Rose stared at him, her jaw slack.

"Umm, that cannot be good, Rose. Is that a nay?"

She continued to stare, though this time he noticed the wetness gathering in the corners of her eyes.

"Please do not cry. I love you with all my heart. We can live wherever you like. I'll love and protect you forever. You'll never have to worry about anyone hurting you again." He kissed her lips again. "Because I'll always be there." He paused for a moment, then added, "If you need to think on it, I can wait a day or two for your answer. You've been through so much in the last fortnight." Hell, but his heart had slowly crept up to his throat as he waited for her answer. He had no idea what she was thinking.

"Aye, Roddy," she whispered. Then she tightened her grip around his neck and leaped into his arms. "Naught would make me happier."

"Rose, you scared the hell out of me. I thought you were about to refuse me." She broke into the widest grin he'd ever seen on her beautiful face. "Och, you are so beautiful, lass."

"I was afraid you'd change your mind." She paused, then added, "I'll admit, I'm afraid I won't belong anywhere but here. I fear I'll not know how other people live. Constance taught me so much. Are you willing to be patient?"

"Without a doubt. You've lived in hell for too long. Did you not know that Clan Grant is its own slice of heaven? A wee bit cold in the winter, but you'll love my clan, if you'll come for a short time. But we can return here if you'd like. 'Tis yours by right."

"Nay." She spun around and stared out over the sea. "I do not wish to live here, but I did wish to come here one last time. My sire's memory will always be in my heart where it belongs."

She breathed deeply and turned back toward the loch to enjoy the beauty of her overlook one last time. The air blew her dark hair away from her face. "I have many fond memories of my sire here, but the other memories are so horrific, I don't know if I could handle it. I wish to be far away from anything that reminds me of my mother. Do you think me weak?"

"Weak? Hellfire, nay. I don't know many people who would have endured such treatment and kept a sound mind. All the lies. The abuse. She was your mother. *Your mother!* You are probably the strongest person I know. Do not ever let yourself think that again."

"Thank you." She turned back to him again, their hands still intertwined. "You helped me through it."

Roddy glanced off into the sky and tipped his head upward. "Someone is here to see you."

She spun around and gazed at her dear owl.

Roddy said, "I don't know if you believe in spirits and such, but I do. I forgot to tell you that your owl followed me down the loch toward the Abbey of Angels. 'Tis why we came back so quickly. That owl could have saved your life."

She dropped Roddy's hand and stepped over to the creature as it landed on the rocky ledge behind her. "Hello. You were quite naughty back there, but Mama deserved every bit of what you gave her. I know exactly why you did it."

The owl rotated its head to the right, then back at her again.

"Do not pretend you don't know what I'm talking about. You did it for me, too. You wanted me to feel as though I didn't need to strike her. You knew if I struck her, I'd live with that for the rest of my life. Despite it all, she was my mother." She blinked several times and touched the talon of one foot. "It worked. That bothered Mama more than any blow I could have delivered. Her heart is one of stone. Many thanks. I have no guilt." She lifted her gaze to the sky.

"I'm so sorry all of that happened to Papa. I so would have loved to have him in in my life forever. I had no memory of the day Mama had caused his death." She stepped closer to the owl, still staring at it. "I know not if you're my sire's spirit or if he sent you, but I'll give you a message to take to him, because I want him to understand. I know this may upset you, but I don't wish to live here any longer. Mama hurt me too much. I want to get as far away as possible." The bird stared at her with big eyes, suddenly looking more orange than gold. Roddy could swear it had understood every word—and that her father had heard her as well. As if receiving a message from on high, the owl lifted one of his talons and waved it—*go on*, it might have said—before he dropped it back onto the ledge. Then he leaned forward and set his beak on her shoulder.

"Thank you. I hope you'll follow me to Grant land."

The owl leaned back, stared at her, and tipped his head. Then he spread his wings and soared into the sky.

Connor called up to them from the caves. "Roddy!"

Since they stood at the highest point of the cliffs above the caves, they had to move closer to hear what he had to say. "Will and Maggie are meeting a magistrate with Rose's mother and her steward to see what other information they can glean from them. The men on the boats are being taken along, also. Rose, do you have anything else you wish to say to her before she goes?"

"Nay, I've said all I have to say. Thank you."

"Constance is going back to the abbey to gather her things," Connor added. "Daniel, Gavin, and Gregor are escorting her. Is there anything you want from there?" Connor climbed up to meet them so they wouldn't have to shout to be heard. He whistled. "'Tis quite a view from up here."

"Nay, I don't need anything. Constance will bring me my few personal effects. My thanks." She leaned against Roddy, still unable to believe they would get married.

Roddy said, "And the others?"

"My guess is it will take about an hour to get the other lasses back to the abbey. Uncle Brodie, Braden, and I will bring them there once they're ready. Rose, are you staying here?"

She shook her head, wrapping her arms around Roddy's waist. "Nay, Roddy has asked me to marry him, and I have accepted. I'll be ready to leave shortly. Mayhap an hour? I'd like to change out of these wet clothes."

Connor clasped Roddy's shoulders and said to both, "Congratulations! Then can you meet us at the abbey in mayhap two hours?"

"Aye, I'll have everything together by then."

"If you have too much, we can split it up into several saddle bags. We have plenty of horses. Shall we leave you one?"

Rose shook her head. "Many of my belongings are at the abbey. We'll be fine."

Connor waved and strode back through the caves to the castle.

After he left, Roddy said, "Shall we gather your things?"

"Aye, but also I wish for us to become a married couple."

He took a step closer, running the back of his fingers down one cheek. "Rose, do you understand what it is that married couples do? Do you know how bairns are made?"

Rose blushed the deepest shade of pink he'd ever seen. He was going to have to be extremely gentle with his wee lovebird.

CHAPTER TWENTY-THREE

———◆———

ROSE COULD FEEL THE BLUSH cover her entire body, but she would not allow her uncertainty to change anything. She loved this man with all her heart, and she wished to be joined with him. Being in his arms was the most pleasing experience she'd ever had.

"Constance explained it to me. While I don't understand it all, I trust you completely, Roddy. Aye, I want this. I want *you*, and I'd prefer for us to lie together here for the first time. I believe we'll find it empty. My mother and Harold have been taken away. Who is left?"

Roddy took a deep breath and said, "We shall check to be certain when we go inside. I understand your reasoning, but if we do this, I would like for us to marry quickly at the abbey. I'll not risk your reputation by waiting. My honor as a Grant warrior won't allow it."

"I agree if 'tis what you want."

"Aye, 'tis my desire to make you mine as soon as possible." He took her hand but pointed for her to lead the way.

Rose helped him navigate the cliffs and the cave and then led him up through the keep to her chamber. When she passed through the hall, she did so as if she had a mask covering her face, not wishing to see any evidence of what had happened. Of the darkness that had unfolded in this place that had been her home.

Roddy said, "The priest's body is gone already, lass."

Once they were in inside her chamber, Roddy started a fire in the hearth. Since he wasn't watching her, she felt brave enough to quickly lift her gown over her head. That done, she removed her shift and climbed into her bed, slipping under the covers before he could see her. Having a man, even the one who was to be her husband, see her in her bare skin made her uncomfortable, though Constance had insisted it was the way of marriage. Her other insistence was that it would be painful for her the first time they coupled. After that, she'd promised, could be pleasant.

She'd also explained how much men loved it.

How she prayed Constance was telling the truth. Enduring a wee bit of pain in order to make Roddy happy was something she would do gladly.

She lay flat on her back and brought the covers up to her chin, folding her hands across her belly. The chamber was still dark, though dawn would be coming soon.

Once Roddy had the fire going, he turned back to look for her, and she could tell he was surprised to find her already in bed. But this man she loved began to slowly remove his own clothing, acting as if this were normal and they'd already been a married couple for years.

She closed her eyes to be polite, but when she peeked out, he was nearly ready to climb into bed. While she'd expected to be frightened by his body, instead she was pleased.

The man she loved was the most handsome man she'd ever met, but now she appreciated what had been hidden underneath his tunic and plaid all along. Roddy's chest was built of sheer muscle, the sprinkling of chest hair following a pattern down across his flat abdomen and then his legs. She'd never seen a man's private area before, so she couldn't stop herself from staring.

Roddy gave her a wry smile when he caught her staring. "I'd ask you if you like what you're seeing, but I fear you may be a little shocked. Your life has been quite protected. I promise you we will fit quite nicely. 'Tis my job to be certain we do. Do not worry about it."

She brought her gaze up to meet his. How had he

guessed what she was thinking? "I trust you, Roddy."

He lifted the coverlet and climbed in next to her. "Later, I will wish to see your beauty, but I respect your modesty this night. You are sure you still want this, Rose?"

"Aye, more than anything. I wish to feel our love. 'Tis how Constance explained it to me." She did her best to hide her fine tremors, though she feared he'd noticed.

"If you change your mind, you only need to stop me and we'll end it."

"I'd rather have you kiss me."

He laced his fingers through her hair and leaned over her, bringing his lips to hers. His lips were soft and warm, so she parted her lips, hoping he would tease her with his tongue as he'd done before. Oh, how she loved being this close to him.

He made her feel special and loved and desired—all things she'd had little enough of in her life before now.

He angled his mouth over hers and delved deeper, his tongue searching for hers, and she followed his lead. Lifting his head, he trailed kisses down her cheek to her neck. "Rose, I want to feel your breasts, taste them," he whispered. "Don't be frightened."

His hands cupped her breasts and his thumb tweaked one nipple, causing strange sensations to race through her. Her body took over, doing things she never would have expected, arching closer to him. An odd whimpering came from her own throat, and Roddy groaned.

"Rose, do you have any idea what the sound of your voice does to me? Those sweet sounds tell me that my Rose is a passionate woman." He took her breast in his mouth, suckling her as she clung to him and cried out his name. He did the same to her other breast until she writhed underneath him, unsure of what was happening inside of her.

"What is it you wish for me to do? Just tell me, love."

She rasped, "I don't know. Do whatever gives you pleasure. I want more, but I cannot describe what or how…"

He chuckled and his hand slipped down to the vee in her legs. "Rose, you are ready for me," he said huskily. "This will hurt at first, but then 'twill get better. Do you trust me?" He stopped to gaze into her eyes, and she was so lost in the love she saw there, the desire for something more burning inside her, that all she could do was nod.

Roddy grasped her hips and settled himself between her legs. She felt his hardness against her, the velvety surface teasing her entrance. He slid the tip inside her just a bit, and she spread her legs because she wanted him closer. As soon as she opened wider, he thrust inside and she felt a small pinch.

He stopped, panting for control. Sweat covered his brow, but he still held her, his skin touching her everywhere in a way that was so sensual, so primal, she didn't wish to stop. "I'm sorry, Rose."

She moved against him, drawing him in and out, and said, "I'm not. More, Roddy."

Roddy closed his eyes and moaned, grabbing her hips and plunging into her with a wild abandon she loved, picking up his pace until an overbearing sense of need threatened to explode inside her. She wiggled a bit to get him to hit her just right, and after a few more thrusts, she held her breath and exploded, plunging into an abyss she hadn't known existed. Roddy shouted her name, grunting his pleasure.

She clung to him, stunned at what they'd just shared, at how much this man meant to her. He kissed her brow and said, "Am I hurting you still?"

"Nay, Roddy you could never hurt me." Her finger traced his jawline, the golden stubble there rough against her finger, yet she loved it. "I think we shall have a most wonderful life together."

Once they arrived at the abbey, Connor and Daniel greeted them, explaining that the others had returned to Braden's keep. They filled them in on everything that had taken place.

Connor said, "There's a visiting priest here to assist for a fortnight until they find a new one. The lasses have been returned, and they are all grateful for our assistance, though many of them slept through much of the ordeal. Once we explained where they were headed, their fear knew no bounds. The abbess claims to have had no knowledge of any of this, stating that it all took place at Father Seward's Abbey of Angels, somewhere she was not welcome. Rose, she did confirm that your mother was the wealthy bene-factor who gave the priest the coin to build the new abbey, one he would have sole control of, which he was excited about. The abbess didn't know anything about an English-man, unfortunately. We questioned some of the monks, but they didn't know his name, said he'd disappeared.

"Father Seward apparently did not like dealing with the abbess, who is sick to learn about what he did with some of the lasses. Maggie and Will plan to investigate every-thing with the magistrate, I'm sure. They'll probably go to the king with what they learn."

Rose asked, "Is Constance here? I need to see her."

"Aye," Daniel said. "She's here, and she's opted to stay. We did our best to convince her to come to Clan Grant with us, but she has refused. Mayhap she'll listen to you."

Rose turned to Roddy and asked, "Would you mind if I speak with her alone?"

"Nay, go ahead." He took her hand and squeezed it. "I'll search out that priest."

"Why?" Daniel asked, his brow furrowing.

"Rose and I are getting married, right now. I don't wish to wait."

Connor nodded. "I think 'tis a brilliant idea. You'll only be delayed by everyone at Clan Grant." Then he glanced at

Rose. "That is, if 'tis what you both want."

Rose stood on her tiptoes to plant a kiss on Roddy's lips. "I've never wanted anything more."

"Come," Daniel said, "I'll take you to Constance while Connor takes Roddy to the priest. After all that's happened, they've allowed us free travel inside the abbey for two days. Much will be changing around here."

They found Constance in an odd place, just coming out of the chapel.

As soon as the lasses exchanged greetings, Daniel said, "I'll go check on that priest."

Rose could see the wetness on her cheeks and knew her dearest friend had been crying. "Constance? What's wrong? Are you not happy about all that has happened?"

Constance launched herself at her for a big hug. "Rose, you know I could not be happier for you. You can hear and you can speak and I adore you. You have everything that I've dreamed of—a man who loves you, a new clan. I feel terrible about all your mother forced you to endure. What a horrible woman." She huffed a deep breath strong enough to move a curl that had been over her eyes. "My mother was always overwhelmed because there were so many of us, but I always knew she loved me."

"Constance, do not worry about me. I am in love with Roddy and he has asked me to marry him. Will you stand by my side when we marry on the morrow?"

Her friend grabbed her hands and hopped up and down. "Oh, Rose. I'm so happy for you! Aye, I wouldn't miss it."

"Come to Clan Grant with us. I was hoping you would join us, find a new place to start fresh. Mayhap you'll meet someone there. Marry and start your own family."

Constance sighed deeply, then took Rose's hand and marched over to the back of the chapel, tugging her behind her. "I cannot explain it, but all of a sudden, my heart is saying mayhap I should take my vows. When I think of all the evil in the world, and of a lass coming here who has been treated the way you were, I cannot help but think mayhap I can be of use here." She stared at the altar, then glanced back at her friend. "I'm just not sure yet, so I'd like to stay here for a time. But if I change my mind and feel I don't belong, I'll come visit you."

"Promise?"

Constance embraced her friend. "I promise. Though first I wish to find Daniel so he'll tell me about what happened to his arm. He promised."

Daniel stuck his head back around the corner and said, "Nay. I'll not tell unless you're at Clan Grant." Then he smiled at Rose. "Now, she must come to visit you."

Daniel disappeared and Rose whispered to her friend, "You must come. I think Daniel likes you."

Constance teared up and said, "That won't matter to me."

Rose wondered what her friend meant by that statement, but Roddy came to get them to meet the priest.

She'd probably never know.

———————◆———————

Roddy and Rose married at the abbey the next morn, outside near the hedge in the back. Connor and Daniel stayed at Roddy's side, while Constance stood by Rose.

Right after the ceremony began, they were both pleased to see an owl soar over them before it landed on the branch above the bench.

The priest had asked, "Does that owl bother you?"

They shook their head in unison and Roddy said, "Not at all. Please continue."

CHAPTER TWENTY-FOUR

WHEN THEY FINALLY ARRIVED AT Clan Grant, Roddy could feel the fine tremors in Rose's body, so he gave her waist a squeeze and whispered, "You'll love it here. You'll see."

A few horses headed in their direction. They were soon joined by Jamie, Jake, Padraig, and Magnus. Roddy whispered, "I'll introduce you when we arrive at the stables."

They dismounted near the stables and were greeted by several Grants: Roddy introduced Jake and Jamie to Rose as the lairds of her new clan, and they offered her a warm welcome. The others lingered to make the journey with them, assisting them with their belongings.

Roddy's sire quickly set Rose at ease with his kind manner. "Welcome to you, Rose," he said, "we are so pleased to have you here with us. This is Roddy's brother Padraig and Ashlyn's husband, Magnus." While Uncle Alex could be intimidating, his father and Uncle Brodie were both as easy-going as could be.

When Roddy caught Rose staring at Magnus's arms, he said, "They don't come any bigger than Magnus, but he has a heart as soft as any lass. Don't let his size scare you." Magnus pretended to glare at Roddy, but he couldn't hold the glum look for long. He broke into a warm smile and said, "Welcome, Rose."

Roddy's father clapped him on the back. "Your mother awaits us in the keep." Once they arrived, Roddy introduced his mother to Rose. "I'm so pleased to have you here," she said. "I want you to know I came here on my own just as you did, scared to death of all these giant men, and I brought two wee lassies with me. Everyone was as kind as could be. You will love it here."

Roddy gave them a sheepish look and said, "I need to tell you something, Mama and Papa. Rose and I fell in love, and since we were at the abbey, we had a visiting priest marry us."

His parents appeared stunned, but they recovered quickly, smiling and hugging them both.

"I apologize," Rose said, "but I had a dear friend who decided to stay at the abbey, and I wished to have her by my side."

His mother said, "That makes perfect sense. Though I am surprised, I couldn't be more pleased. You and Roddy seem verra happy. Come inside and sit by the hearth. We'll get you something to eat."

"Well," his sire said, "we'll have to find a place for you two to live. I suppose you can live with us for a bit, but I'm guessing you'd like your own place. I'll go talk with our lairds." His mother left with him to find food for them.

Gracie came running down the stairs, headed straight for them. "Roddy! I'm so glad to see you! And I see you've brought someone with you. Introduce us, please."

"This is my wife, Rose. We've decided to live at Clan Grant, so we're hoping everyone will welcome us."

"Married? You, Roddy? I'm so surprised, but so happy for you." She gave Rose a quick hug and said, "My brother is wonderful. You chose well. I'm excited to have another sister."

"I'll admit I'm anxious," Rose said. "My life has been quite different than Roddy's."

Earning her name, Gracie said, "I cannot wait to hear all about it, but please excuse me for a moment. I'm worried about my brother. Roddy, are those nightmares still bothering you?"

Roddy pulled up a chair for Gracie so the three of

them sat down together. As she made herself comfortable, he looked over at Rose. He hadn't given the matter any thought, but he realized he hadn't had a nightmare in quite some time. "Nay, the dreams haven't troubled me since I jumped in the loch to help Rose."

"Good, I'm glad. I was worried after you left. I apologize I didn't talk to you more about it. Papa said you don't remember it at all. Mayhap I can help you."

Roddy said, "It took quite a while for me to remember what happened. Bits and pieces returned to me, but not all of it. I did recall finding you underwater. But how did you get tangled in the net so deep?"

Gracie raised her eyebrows. "You do not remember?"

"Nay. I remember Da saving us, but I don't remember how it all started."

Gracie reached over and placed her hand on his forearm. "I tell you this only to help you understand your nightmares. You pushed me in. 'Twas all in good fun, as we often pushed each other into the water. You came running out of the cottage and shoved me so hard I flew in an odd direction."

Roddy couldn't have been more shocked at this revelation. He had no memory of pushing her at all. No wonder he'd had bad dreams about the incident for so long.

He was to blame.

His dear sister could have died because of his foolish actions.

Gracie must have seen the emotions play across his face. "Roddy, I forgave you long ago. We were young, and 'twas the way we all played on the loch. In fact, it earned you that small scar above your eye. Please do not think on it for another moment." She stood and leaned down to kiss his forehead. Then she reached over and squeezed Rose's hand. "Welcome to the family, Rose, and my congratulations to both of you on your wedding. I wish you much happiness."

"By the way, Rose. You'll be an aunt to the bairn Gracie and Jamie are expecting early spring." Roddy turned his attention to his sister. "Gracie, you'll make a wonderful mother."

"My thanks, brother." She lifted her hand in a wave and headed out the front door.

He looked at Rose and grabbed both of her hands, squeezing them. "Guilt. 'Twas all guilt."

Rose added, "And you were able to block it all out in order to save me. I doubt your nightmares will come back."

———————

Rose stood on the end of the loch, staring at their new cottage. "Roddy, 'tis beautiful. I love it. Your clan built it so quickly. I'm so grateful."

She remembered they day they'd arrived at Clan Grant.

Rose had been so taken by the sight of Grant Castle that it had nearly moved her to tears. The keep boasted at least six towers and the curtain wall had the most impressive parapets she'd ever seen. She'd been surprised by the number of people who had come out to greet them from the village, waving and shouting to welcome them home. Much of the land was hilly and rocky, so there weren't many fields, but the ones they had were carefully tended.

Bright flowers had abounded near every home, the rich colors of autumn catching her by surprise. Leaves and branches had stood braided and interwoven on the doors or the front gates, nearly as welcoming as the smiles on everyone's face.

She had been petrified that she would never be able to fit into such a majestic place, but she couldn't have been more wrong. Everyone had welcomed her, and now they had their own home.

Roddy came over and wrapped his arms around her, leaning his head on hers as they both stared at their new place. "We don't have the regal cliffs of your home, but I love being near the water. We can raise our own bairns here, teach them to swim."

"Aye, just as my sire did with me."

"This spot is perfect. My parents are not far, my sister Ashlyn and her family are just down the hill, and the area my uncle built for swimming is at the other end.

She tipped her head back and kissed his chin. "No more nightmares, no more guilt. Not for either of us."

"Nay, not since I fell in love with you, Rose," he said. "You are the best thing that ever happened to me."

They stared at their new home for a few more moments when Roddy let go of her and said, "Wait! I forgot something. I built it for you. I'll be right back."

He raced over to the building that served as both a stable and a place for storage. After retrieving the ungainly object, he tore back across the path and said, "We had extra wood, so I made this for you."

Rose looked at the T-shaped creation, wishing to share his obvious excitement, but she had no idea what it was. "Roddy, I can see 'twas quite an effort, but I have no idea what 'tis."

Roddy held up one finger, a request for her to wait, then found a shovel and dug a hole, sticking the long pole down deep and covering it with tightly packed dirt. The T-section was on top.

She waited patiently, hoping she'd discover the thing's purpose, but she simply could not. She had to admit to her failings. "What is it?" she asked, feeling horrible that she didn't understand.

He scowled and said, "'Tis a perch."

He glanced up into the sky and said, "Give it a few minutes." He came to her side and pointed up in the sky.

Sure enough, an owl appeared overhead several minutes later, soaring freely in the wind. Then it aimed straight for them and landed directly on the new perch.

Rose said, "Greetings, my friend."
The owl lifted its wings once and said, "Hoo."

EPILOGUE

Spring, 1285

ALEXANDER GRANT STOOD BENEATH THE large hearth in the great hall of his clan's castle, his hands on his hips as he stared up at the weaponry above the hearth.

His brother Robbie joined him. "Could be a big day, brother."

"Aye, 'struth, Robbie. Most of all, I pray 'twill be a healthy and happy day for all. Or should I say, a happy sennight. Bairns have minds of their own, as you well know. They'll be here when they're ready and not a moment before."

"Truer words have never been spoken. Papa would be proud."

A grin crossed Alex's face as he thought about their beloved sire. He'd been strict with his sons, but they'd always known the man with the gruff bark had the softest heart of all, especially when it came to their mother.

"I like the way Jamie and Jake arranged the weaponry," Robbie said, his gaze cresting the wide stone hearth. The mantel was covered with aromatic candles amid dried greens and berries carefully tied with ribbons by Maddie and Celestina. The various daggers, swords, and knives were mounted on the wall. The tapestries depicting the castle in the four seasons, which his mother had made so long ago, still decorated the long wall of the hall. Though their castle had grown in size, with added towers and a third story, they'd kept many things from the original keep.

"Aye, they did a nice job. Papa would be pleased to see

some of his finest swords hanging there for all to see. If only Maddie hadn't insisted I clean the blood from them," Alex said, a bit of remorse in his tone.

"Your sword belongs above the others. Do you think the laddie destined to lift that mighty sword will be born today?"

Alex grasped his brother's shoulder. "I can only hope the bairn is healthy and will bring us new joy."

A woman's voice echoed behind him. "You do not fool me at all, dear brother. You wish to have another wee lassie to strap to your chest," Alex's sister Brenna said.

Alex pulled her close so he could kiss her forehead. "I hope you have a fine day, sister, and may the Lord guide your gifted hands."

***

Upon learning the news that the babes were due at around the same time, Alex had summoned his sisters, both renowned healers, to assist Caralyn with the births. Shortly after Brenna had arrived with her husband Quade, their sister Jennie, also the baby of the family, had arrived with her entire family in tow. Alex hadn't waited long before summoning the elders into his solar to tell them the news.

"Sisters," he'd announced, barely able to keep a straight face. "I have information for you that is only known by a chosen few. Maddie and Caralyn both know the truth, as do a few others, but I do not wish this to be shared widely until the time arrives for certes."

Jennie had given Brenna a strange look, but they'd waited for Alex to tell the full tale.

"As you will surely learn, Jamie and Finlay have been unbearable in their constant competition about which one will have the first laddie of the next generation of my heirs. They've been so obnoxious about it that both Gracie and Kyla have forbidden them to discuss it in front of the two of them."

Aedan and Quade both burst into laughter at about the same time.

"The lists must be something to watch," Aedan said.

Jennie stilled her husband by placing her hand over his. "I'd like to hear what else Alex has to say. I think there's a reason he called both of us here. After all, there are now three healers here to tend two women who may not deliver together at all."

Jennie tipped her head as she watched her brother's expression. "Out with it, dearest brother." Alex had been like a father to Jennie, so he often gave in to her whims, even at this age.

"Verra astute of you, Jennie. Because of their competitiveness, Jake has made us all promise to keep his secret."

Both sisters gasped at the same time, the excitement and disbelief on their faces contagious.

Brenna reached for Quade's hand and squeezed it. "Three? Aline is carrying, too?"

Alex didn't attempt to hide his own excitement over the news. Though he had learned to hide his emotions when need be, this he could not control.

He nodded slowly, waggling his brow at them. "Caralyn said all three are due at about the same time."

Jennie squealed as he'd known she would, but then she sat and whispered, "Bairns make their own decisions about leaving the womb. While it would be exciting to have them deliver close together, the odds are slim."

Alex nodded. "Understood, but I didn't wish to take the risk. Please keep Jake and Aline's secret until the time arrives. If you don't, Jamie and Finlay will be even more unbearable, and I do not wish to upset a wee woman in her last month of carrying. Aline has done her best to stay hidden, claiming illness, and has worn oversized gowns for some time now. No one has suspected anything as of yet."

That meeting had been six days ago, and the time had finally come today. Gracie had been dealing with pains for a short time, and Kyla had called for her mother and Caralyn to check her. Both had been put in two chambers with access to the balcony in case they were in need of anything.

Word had apparently traveled quickly, as the door to the keep continued to open, even though it was the middle of the night. Roddy and Rose were the latest arrivals.

"Gracie is ready?" Roddy directed the question to his father while he helped Rose with her mantle.

"Aye, we think 'tis her time and possibly Kyla's, as well."

Alex loved having so many of his clan together in the keep.

True, a few of the births in this keep had been difficult, but he had a good feeling about this day. A fabulous feeling.

Alex and Robbie gave instructions for food and drink to be brought in from the kitchens and then built fires in the two hearths, while Quade Ramsay settled in a chair, wearing a big grin as he watched all the chaos.

That done, the gathering began to seem more like a celebration. Alex grabbed an ale and surveyed the chattering group in the hall, their excitement contagious. They were ready for whatever might come, though Alex sensed a bit of tension from Caralyn, Robbie's wife. Was it because it was her daughter who was giving birth, or because the babe might be the next heir to the lairddom?

Alex attempted to calm his sister-in-law. "Brenna is already upstairs with Gracie, Caralyn. Take your time. She said 'twill be a while yet. You know how it can be with new mamas. Kyla insists 'tis time for the bairn to make its appearance, but Maddie mustn't be concerned as of yet. If she were, she'd be at the balcony giving me orders."

Caralyn laughed. "This is a first for both of you. The first grandbairn, and the second at the same time." She rolled her eyes, telling Alex she was also thinking of the third grandbairn, the one who was still a secret.

Just then, Finlay rushed out onto the balustrade with

an urgency that caught everyone's attention. He shouted, "Aunt Brenna, I need Aunt Brenna!"

The entire group in the great hall stopped what they were doing to look at the frantic husband above. Only Caralyn had the presence of mind to act. She hurried up the stairs and asked, "Finlay, what is it?"

"Kyla says she's having the bairn. What should I do?"

The unexpected complication seemed to calm Caralyn more than it did baffle her. "Brenna is busy with Gracie. I'll come check on Kyla." Caralyn climbed the staircase and shepherded a pale Finlay back into his chamber.

Just then Alex's wee wife, still as beautiful as the day they'd married, stepped out onto the balcony. She caught his gaze and gave him an almost imperceptible nod, letting him know it was indeed Kyla's time.

As he stared up at this woman he adored, so many thoughts ran through his mind that he made his way over to the staircase, never taking his gaze off Maddie. Fortunately, she saw him coming and waited for him, a nervous smile on her face.

He'd seen that same smile the day he married her, the day she'd struggled to bring Elizabeth into the world, and the day she sat by his side on the cold ground after he took a sword wound that nearly killed him. Love wasn't a strong enough word to express his feelings for this woman. After all these years, he knew exactly what that smile meant— she was worried about all that was upon them. Their first three bairns were about to become parents, and she feared something would go wrong. He headed up the stairs to give her what comfort he could.

When he reached her side, she gave a slight nod. "I think 'twill be today, Alex."

He noticed the tear in the corner of his tender-hearted wife's eye. He wrapped his arms around her and lifted her off her feet, eliciting the same squeal he'd heard from her many times before. He planted a kiss on her lips, wondering how she could taste more delicious every day. The small roar in the hall beneath them didn't stop him, but he gave in to her sensibilities as he always did, knowing that when he glanced at her, he would see the deep blush covering her face and traveling down her neck. He slid her back down his body and she whispered, "Alex, they're all watching." He let out a small Grant war whoop and clapped his hands together.

He turned to lean over the balcony railing and shouted for all to hear, "Aye! Two in one day." He couldn't help but lift his gaze to the rafters, a small prayer chanting in his mind to keep all healthy on this momentous day.

Or would it be on the morrow?

He really didn't care.

Maddie said, "I must go back inside. You'll not be offended that Kyla does not want you at her side?"

He spun back around, his eyes wide and his jaw open. "Nay, I'll not be in there." He made his way back down the staircase, enjoying the sight of all his *clann* together.

Quade asked, "Do you think they'll both have them today?"

Alex snorted. "Mayhap they will. The healers have a way of knowing, but I surely don't." Who would have known that the wee woman he'd brought back to his clan so many years ago could have brought him such joy? They'd been blessed so many times over the years and would soon count even more blessings. Today or the morrow, he did not care.

The group in the hall spread out as more and more people arrived to celebrate.

Brodie and Celestina.

Nicol, Finlay's sire.

Fergus and Davina.

As soon as Finlay heard that his brother had come, he flew down the stairs to greet him. Jamie heard their voices, so he joined them down below, leaving his wife for a spell.

And so the bragging and taunting began.

Jamie started. "You just could not let it be, could you, Finlay? Did you sit on Kyla's belly or something? We're having the first laddie. Tell her she can take her time with the lassie. No reason to hurry." He did his best to appear calm, but his sudden need to pace took over. He started a small path near the staircase, his arms crossed in front of his chest.

"You think I would do that to your sister?" Finlay barked. "I'd knock you out, Grant, if not for the fact your wife is about to deliver. You're pacing because Kyla will have our lad first. See if I'm not telling the truth." His hands settled on his hips and he leaned forward, nearly touching his friend each time Jamie paced past him.

"Just not another word, Finlay," Jamie barked.

Robbie grinned at Alex and Brodie. "We can sit here by the hearth and watch this show for days. Wait until Jake shows up, then they'll really get going."

The three brothers pulled a few chairs away from the hearth and turned them to face the two new fathers-to-be, wide grins on their faces.

"Promises to be great entertainment, I say," Alex bellowed. The bickering had continued, unabated by all of the not-so-subtle observers. "We could start wagering. Bring out the coin, lads, if you're so certain of the outcome."

Brodie helped Celestina into a chair while he chatted with his two brothers. "I wouldn't have missed this for anything. Celestina kept telling me to slow down, but I couldn't. Look at Nicol."

Nicol, soon to be a grandpapa, paced behind Finlay, chewing on a thumbnail and glancing up at the door to Kyla's chamber every once in a while.

To everyone's surprise, Jake came barreling out of the tower chamber entrance to the hall, his usual sleeping chamber, carrying Aline cradled in his arms. Aunt Jennie followed him out.

The entire group stopped to stare. Jennie hurried over

to kiss Alex on the cheek. "Oh, dear brother, this is quite a day for you." She chuckled and patted his shoulder as he stared in excitement at Aline. Jennie reached up to close his mouth. "She's a wee bit closer than Caralyn thought. It could be three bairns born on this day."

Roddy said, "I thought she was sick for the last moon."

His father chuckled. "Had to keep the secret, lad, though 'twasn't easy."

Jennie laughed. "Nay, Aline was just carrying a big belly around that she was doing her best to hide in large gowns."

Jake grinned at his brother and Finlay. "We only kept her in hiding so we wouldn't have to listen to you two. 'Twas her choice to stay away from both of you over the last moon. But I could not be more pleased we handled it this way and no one suspected. We'll see who has the first laddie." He carried his wife up the stairs, his shoulders squared, and his deep laugh echoed across the hall.

Finlay and Jamie both ran over to hang onto the railing as Jake carried his wife up the stairs.

"You hid it?"

"You were so afraid of us that you could not tell anyone?"

Jake slowed a bit to reply. "Aye, Aline didn't want you arguing with us about whether we'll have a lad or lassie. We do not care what we have."

A loud boom caught all their attentions. "Lads!" Alex shouted, having just stomped his foot on the floor. "Give the mothers-to-be some peace, please."

Finlay and Jamie both shrunk back from the stair railing. Jamie blushed a bit and whispered, "My apologies, Aline."

Aline replied with a long moan, her hands clenched in fists across her belly. "Hurry, Jake. I know Aunt Jennie wanted us all upstairs together since it seems we're going to have our bairns on the same day, but you need to make haste or I'll have our bairn on the staircase.

Jake traveled the rest of the way up the stairs, taking Aline to a chamber off to the right. Finlay and Kyla were to the far left with Jamie and Gracie's chamber in the middle.

Jennie checked on Kyla first, then emerged long enough to lean over the railing. "Things are progressing well. Maddie and Caralyn have everything under control." She moved down to Gracie's room, then came back out to give them another update. "Gracie is also progressing well. Brenna and Ashlyn have everything under control. I'm going to stay with Aline. Celestina, would you mind assisting me?"

Celestina jumped with delight. "I'd love to."

Moments later, Jake came flying down the stairs and charged over to Jamie and Finlay, the two of them still arguing. He gave Jamie a shove and said, "And that is why Aline and I kept it a secret. I didn't wish for my wife to have to listen to you two. Lad or lassie, I'll love both, though I'm quite sure we'll have the first laddie."

"Hellfire, Jake, that was underhanded," Finlay ran his hand through his dark red hair, sweat dotting his brow. "I didn't know I had to worry about *both* of you. One is hard enough."

Alex sat down in his chair and allowed the banter to continue for a few moments, before he finally ground out, "You're all fools."

In unison, the three fathers-to-be repeated, "What?"

"Why?" Jake asked, bewilderment clear on his face.

"Because your wee wives are up there working harder than they ever have, and you three are down here acting like having a bairn is naught. If you truly wished to show your wife respect, you'd be by her side mopping her brow and holding her hand. I never missed one of my children's births."

The three young men exchanged glances and then took off toward the staircase at the same exact time, shoving at one another along the way.

Brodie said, "They'll never survive this, Alex."

It was the longest night Alex had ever been through,

though the joyous laughter abounded in the great hall and there was much ale consumed. He was nearly as nervous as his wee wife, though he'd never admit it to anyone. Six. He had six clan members to worry about. Three new ones and three lassies giving birth.

At one point, Rose sighed and said, "I just love Clan Grant, husband. They all love each other so much, though they show it in different ways."

Finally, about three hours later, Celestina came out of Jake and Aline's chamber and announced, "It's a wee laddie!"

The door at the opposite end opened and Maddie came out, leaned over the railing and said, "'Tis a laddie!"

Amid the applause and celebration, the third door opened and Ashlyn came out of the chamber, her face tear-stained. "'Tis a wee laddie."

Alex's voice came out as a shout above the others. "Brenna, Caralyn, Jennie!"

All three healers stepped out and Brenna, in the middle of the other two, asked, "What is it, Alex?"

"Which one was first?"

The entire hall turned silent in an instant, awaiting her answer.

Brenna looked at Jennie, who said, "I'd say five minutes ago."

Caralyn shrugged her shoulders. "I'd say the same."

Brenna nodded to the group. "There you have it. All three lads were born at exactly the same time. You'll have to deal with it, Alex. They're all your grandsons." The three healers returned to their chambers to finish their work.

Nothing was said in the hall, everyone waiting for Alex to speak and declare who was his first descendant of the next generation, but he never did.

Jake flew out of his room declaring, "Our laddie was first."

Jamie must have heard him, for he bolted out of his

chamber. "Our laddie is the firstborn."

The door of Kyla and Finlay's chamber opened, and Maddie and Caralyn, assisted by a maid, dragged Finlay out of the chamber. They left him there on the balcony above the hall. Maddie leaned over the edge and said, "Nicol, come get your son. He fainted."

Alex beamed with pride. The crowd around him all awaited his pronouncement. "I couldn't have planned it any better than nature, and I never argue with her."

He ran a hand through his thick hair and said, "Three laddies all born at the exact same time. What a blessing!"

———◆———

And so the story was told for generation after generation.

Alasdair, dark-haired son of Jake (John) Grant and Aline Carron.

Elshander, fair-haired son of Jamie (James) Grant and Gracie Grant, and

Alick, fire-haired son of Kyla Grant and Finlay MacNicol.

All three were born on the same day, at the same exact time, all descendants of the renowned Alexander Grant, the finest swordsman in all the land.

When their time comes, the three shall lead Clan Grant together to be one of the strongest clans in Scottish history.

———◆———

DEAR READERS,

Thanks so much for reading *Highland Lies* and continuing on this journey with me. If you haven't guessed it, Daniel and Constance's story will be next. I just love these two characters.

I haven't enjoyed writing a scene as much as I did the epilogue in a long, long time. I love it whenever I write in Alex's point of view. He's such a great character, if I do say so myself!

The epilogue is total fiction, by the way. I haven't encountered any similar situation in my research. I had no plan to write it until halfway through this novel. The scene between Roddy and Gracie inspired me. Originally, I had only planned on Gracie being pregnant.

And yes, I will be writing a trilogy in the future featuring Alasdair, Elshander, and Alick. Not this year, it's still brewing in my mind, but I hope to write the first of the series in 2019.

Happy reading!

As always, reviews would be greatly appreciated. Sign up for my newsletter on my website at *www.keiramontclair.com*. I send newsletters out with each new release.

Another way to receive notices about my new releases is to follow me on BookBub. Click on the tab in the upper right-hand side of my profile page. You can also write a review on BookBub.

Keira Montclair

www.keiramontclair.com
www.facebook.com/KeiraMontclair
www.pinterest.com/KeiraMontclair

NOVELS BY KEIRA MONTCLAIR

THE BAND OF COUSINS
HIGHLAND VENGEANCE
HIGHLAND ABDUCTION
HIGHLAND RETRIBUTION
HIGHLAND LIES

THE CLAN GRANT SERIES
#1- RESCUED BY A HIGHLANDER-Alex and Maddie
#2- HEALING A HIGHLANDER'S HEART-Brenna and Quade
#3- LOVE LETTERS FROM LARGS-Brodie and Celestina
#4-JOURNEY TO THE HIGHLANDS-Robbie and Caralyn
#5-HIGHLAND SPARKS-Logan and Gwyneth
#6-MY DESPERATE HIGHLANDER-Micheil and Diana
#7-THE BRIGHTEST STAR IN THE HIGH-LANDS-Jennie and Aedan
#8- HIGHLAND HARMONY-Avelina and Drew

THE HIGHLAND CLAN
LOKI-Book One
TORRIAN-Book Two
LILY-Book Three
JAKE-Book Four

ABOUT THE AUTHOR

Keira Montclair is the pen name of an author who lives in Florida with her husband. She loves to write fast-paced, emotional romance, especially with children as secondary characters in her stories.

She has worked as a registered nurse in pediatrics and recovery room nursing. Teaching is another of her loves, and she has taught both high school mathematics and practical nursing.

Now she loves to spend her time writing, but there isn't enough time to write everything she wants! Her Highlander Clan Grant series, comprising of eight standalone novels, is a reader favorite. Her third series, The Highland Clan, set twenty years after the Clan Grant series, focuses on the Grant/Ramsay descendants. She also has a contemporary series set in The Finger Lakes of Western New York and a paranormal historical series, The Soulmate Chronicles.

Her latest series, The Band of Cousins, stems from The Highland Clan but is a stand-alone series.

Contact her through her website, *www.keiramontclair.com*.